TO _____

FROM _____

The great virtues and enduring promises in Scripture are what Hope Valley and *When Calls the Heart* are all about. Brian Bird and Michelle Cox are now sharing those "God moments" with all of us in *When God Calls the Heart*. I love this devotional!

—LEE STROBEL, best-selling author of *The Case for Christ*

I am a devoted fan of the television series *When Calls the Heart*, so I know for a fact that anyone who loves this series as much as I do will want this exceptional book for their personal collection. It offers not only daily inspiration but poignant moments to ponder as well as sweet reminders of favorite scenes from a beloved cast of characters.

—BEVERLY LEWIS, *New York Times* best-selling author

So proud of my partner Brian Bird and coauthor Michelle Cox for these beautiful little booster shots of hope in *When God Calls the Heart*. If you're feeling cynical about the world right now, this book will cure you!

— MICHAEL LANDON JR., executive producer and cocreator of *When Calls the Heart* and the *Love Comes Softly* series

A lovely devotional. The perfect companion for the many fans of *When Calls the Heart*.

—FRANCINE RIVERS, *New York Times* best-selling author

Hearties are going to find encouragement and inspiration tucked away in the pages of this Hope Valley treasure!

—TODD STARNES, best-selling author and host of *The Todd Starnes Show* on Fox News Radio

This book of devotionals is a delight. Brian Bird and Michelle Cox have succeeded in capturing the spirit that resonates through all of Janette Oke's stories. The thoughtful and caring nature that impacts readers around the globe shines from these pages. Highly recommended.

—DAVIS BUNN, internationally best-selling author

I hadn't quite jumped on the bandwagon when everyone around me started celebrating the television series *When Calls the Heart*. And I admit that in spite of the fact that Brian Bird is one of the folks I'm proud to call friend. Then, one day I tuned in to season 1, episode 1. Several episodes later, I penned a quick note to Brian that roughly said, *I'm hooked, and I may never get back to work.* Now, another dear friend, Michelle Cox, has joined forces with Brian to write this book of devotions. The words are beautifully penned, and the messages are clear and poignant. Even not-yet-Hearties will want this book as an addition to their daily reading.

—EVA MARIE EVERSON, award-winning speaker and best-selling author, including *The One True Love of Alice-Ann*

A growing army of fans—the Hearties—have come to love the world of *When Calls the Heart*. Now let the show's cocreator, Brian Bird, along with inspirational writer Michelle Cox, introduce you to a *spiritual* world behind the TV series. Their daily readings will remind you to slow down, look up, and reach out to the One who gave us our hearts in the first place—and who wants to keep them close to His.

—MARK MITTELBERG, best-selling author of *Confident Faith*
and *The Case for Christ Devotional* (with Lee Strobel)

The art of storytelling, when used for the purpose of revealing timeless and life-changing truths, brings an effortless and welcomed transformation that both realigns and reinvigorates the soul. It's like a melody specifically honed for readers, as if they are the only ones meant to be touched. Such is what I have found in *When God Calls the Heart*.

—CAMY "CAMERON" ARNETT, minister and entrepreneur,
and cohost and producer of *The Christian View*; CamyArnett.com

If you consider yourself a "Heartie" or not, *When God Calls the Heart* is an exquisitely crafted devotional that will bring out the rich resolve in each of us. Brian Bird and my dear friend Michelle Cox have extracted the very best out of this well-loved story and have written a devotional that will transport you right to the heart of Hope Valley. You will renew your warm friendship with Elizabeth, learn from the wisdom of Abigail Stanton, long to be a mother to little Cody, and laugh in good-natured frustration at Rosemary Coulter. *When God Calls the Heart* is a devotional that makes time travel possible, prayer more meaningful, and the principles of God jump right off the page.

—CAROL MCLEOD, best-selling author and speaker;
author of *Let There Be Joy*!

We all have favorite settings and characters that remain in our hearts even after the stories are finished. With this book, we don't have to say goodbye to the gentle wisdom and heartfelt faith that makes *When Calls the Heart* such an amazing phenomenon. The applications found in this devotional are rock solid and the takeaways profound.

—EDIE MELSON, award-winning author and blogger, director of
the Blue Ridge Mountains Christian Writers Conference

When God Calls the Heart is an invitation for God to open your heart and your eyes to how He works in the everyday and to be filled with excitement for when, where, and how He is using you!

—ERICA WIGGENHORN, speaker and author of *An Unexplainable Life:
Recovering the Wonder and Devotion of the Early Church* and *The Unexplainable Church:
Rediscovering the Mission of the Early Believers*

FOREWORD BY JANETTE OKE

WHEN GOD CALLS

the

HEART

DEVOTIONS FROM HOPE VALLEY

Brian Bird & Michelle Cox

BroadStreet
PUBLISHING

BroadStreet Publishing® Group, LLC

Racine, Wisconsin, USA

BroadStreetPublishing.com

WHEN GOD CALLS THE HEART: DEVOTIONS FROM HOPE VALLEY

Stock or custom editions of BroadStreet Publishing titles may be purchased in bulk for educational, business, ministry, fundraising, or sales promotional use. For information, please email info@broadstreetpublishing.com.

Cover design by Garborg Design and based on a painting by Jordan Blackstone. Typesetting by Katherine Lloyd at theDESKonline.com.

Printed in China

18 19 20 21 22   5 4 3 2 1

"You will seek me
and find me
when you seek me
with all your heart."

Jeremiah 29:13

CONTENTS

Foreword by Janette Oke vii

1 Dream Big ... Expect Surprises 1

2 Eviction Notices 5

3 From Guilt to Grace 9

4 A Whale of a Problem 13

5 Life Goes On 17

6 Love Is Tricky 21

7 If You Bake It, They Will Come 25

8 You Are More Than Enough 29

9 Clear as Mud 33

10 Regret Me Not 37

11 Proceed with Caution 41

12 Large and in Charge 45

13 The Cure for Everything 49

14 If the Lace-Up Boot Fits 53

15 Not the Last Resort 57

16 Let Go of the Tree Trunk 61

17 Take No for an Answer 65

18 Spiritual Tooth Decay 69

19 Welcome to the Human Race 73

20 Just Ask 77

21 "Auld Lang Syne" 81

22 Not If ... But When 85

23 Wanted 89

24 Be Someone's Hero 93

25 Loving the Unlovely 97

26 Your One Thing 101

27 The Better Yes 105

28 Heavenly Salve 109

29 The Best Place to Be 113

30 The Perfect Medicine 117

31 Getting Past the Past 121

32 Become a Champion to Someone 125

33 The Most Dangerous Prayer 129

34 Adversity Doesn't Define Us 133

35 Honey, Not Vinegar 137

36 Take a Walk with Me 141

37 Be the Miracle 145

38 Sorry Is the Hardest Word ... 149

39 Less Stressed, More Blessed 153

40 The Two Greatest Virtues ... 157

Parting Words 161

Acknowledgments 163

About the Authors 166

*A*ctually, the only way I *could* look was up. However, "looking up" hardly described my present attitude.

I had taken a tumble on a small patch of ice and was now in an emergency room, flat on my back, waiting for an ambulance trip to the city hospital where I would undergo hip surgery. The medication had barely taken the sharp edge off the pain as I lay staring at the colorless ceiling above me. This had not been in my Sunday morning plans.

My best option was prayer. "Lord, what is this all about? What do you want to accomplish through this little mishap? Help me not to miss it."

Life is filled with bumps. We all experience them. Some are mere inconveniences, others are life-changing. It is so easy to say that God allows them to build our faith—to make us stronger—to show others that God really can and does see us through the tough spots. All the statements are true, but a little hard to keep in mind when we are in the midst of a bump-time.

In the writer's world, we are advised to "write what you know." I've had enough bumps along the way to know something about them. I've also observed the bumps others have received. It seems few, if any of us, are bump-free. I kept that in mind as I wrote my stories of the pioneer people. It seemed that everything about their daily lives was bundled in difficulty. I also remembered the many joys, the blessings, and the treasures that life brings through family and friends, and the answered prayers. The producers of the much-loved films also have "real life" in mind as they guide the able portrayers of the story characters through carefully orchestrated scenes to give us, not just the words, but the faces, the actions, the emotional struggles and tensions of the people of Hope Valley.

As I visited the Town, a privilege for which I am deeply grateful, I thought, *Wow! I never knew it took so many, many people to produce a film.* They were everywhere, busily looking after their given assignments. A wonderful team had been brought together to use their various talents to help us share the lives of ordinary people in ordinary circumstances but with extra-ordinary faith and endurance. Talents come in various sizes, shapes, and intensities. When they are all working toward the same goal, we have "magic." Add the wonderful Hearties fans and you could have a small city. An exciting city. They can get rather boisterous in their enthusiasm. Bless them! They push the whole process forward.

And now, a Hope Valley devotional. One more way to add talent to talent—all to the glory of God. We may see ourselves on one or more pages. Thankfully, the authors do not just speak of the bumps, but lead us to explore the best way to deal with them. And we get to share some heart-warming victories too. Thank you, Brian and Michelle.

Though I treasure the entire Scriptures, there are cherished verses that I have carried for many years, not just in my head, but in my heart. They apply to each of us. One of them is Proverbs 3:5–6: "Trust in the Lord with all your heart and lean not on your own understanding. In all your ways acknowledge Him and He will direct your paths" (NKJV). Translated into my own words—needed because I am still working to practice them—I hear this: really and totally trust God who has proven over and over that He is more than adequate to handle every situation, and don't even bother to try to muddle through situations in your own limited wisdom or ability. In everything, recognize and admit that He is God—all-knowing, all-powerful, loving, and gracious—and only He knows what is best for you, and He will lead you if you let go and put your unwavering faith in Him.

—Janette Oke

1

DREAM BIG ... EXPECT SURPRISES

"For I know the plans I have for you," declares the LORD,
"plans to prosper you and not to harm you,
plans to give you hope and a future."

JEREMIAH 29:11

"I can do this.
We can do whatever God calls us to do—
with His help."
—*Elizabeth Thatcher*

*E*lizabeth Thatcher beamed as she watched the passing beauty of the countryside out the window of her stage coach west. She had big dreams for her future. She couldn't wait to get to her new classroom in Coal Valley and to meet her new students. Elizabeth knew she would have to make some adjustments from her life of privilege back home in the big city, but she planned to face this adventure with courage and dignity.

Lost in her thoughts, she visualized the Coal Valley townspeople welcoming her with excitement, and the children waiting eagerly in their seats in the schoolhouse. The day couldn't get here soon enough.

But in that way that dreams sometimes unravel like yarn from a knitting needle, it didn't happen exactly like that. Elizabeth didn't envision a band of thieves waiting around the next bend for her. She didn't realize they would rob her of everything she had brought west. And instead of her triumphant entry into Coal Valley, she arrived limping, dirty, and bedraggled, hitching a ride in the back of a wagon. The thieves had stolen her dignity as well as her belongings.

Her welcome to Coal Valley wasn't what she'd imagined either. Instead of open arms and excitement, she was greeted with looks of skepticism and comments of derision. Coal Valley was no place for a princess. This was a hard luck town beset by tragedy—a coal mine accident that resulted in many of the children becoming fatherless, and a church fire that left the saloon as the only place to hold school.

And Elizabeth soon discovered that she wasn't prepared

for the primitive living conditions in Coal Valley. An out-house and wood-burning stove in the little teacherage she was meant to live in would mean an uncomfortable new lifestyle. None of it was what she'd expected when she set out to fulfill the big dreams God had put on her heart.

It's that way for all of us, isn't it? Do you have a big dream for your life? A giant goal? A worthy aspiration? Perhaps even something you believe God is calling you to do? It's all very exciting as you begin the journey—but it's easy to forget that life can sometimes derail your dreams or delay your timelines.

As Elizabeth learned, people can discourage us and cir-cumstances can temporarily defeat us, but God never wants us to give up on the dreams He has for us. There is no such thing as being uncalled. We don't get to un-ring that bell—even when the world puts thieves and outhouses in our path.

Persistence always beats resistance.

Prayer from the Heart

Father, I'm grateful for the big plans you've given me, but sometimes the waiting seems so hard. The bumps of life and hardships I face are discouraging. If I'm honest, there are days when I'm ready to quit ... to say that it's too hard ... to say that it isn't worth it. Remind me that even though I can't see what you're doing behind the scenes, you are in charge, you have my future in your hands, and you will equip me with everything I need to achieve what you have put in front of me. Thank you for entrusting me with this big dream. Help me to be faithful to your call.

⌘

What's on Your Heart Today?

- Why do you have trouble trusting God with the big plans He gives you?

- Why is it important to remain faithful, even when things become tough?

- How can you recognize if your big dreams are from God, or if they are just your own desires?

2

EVICTION NOTICES

Though one may be overpowered,
two can defend themselves.
A cord of three strands is not quickly broken.

ECCLESIASTES 4:12

"You have every right to be afraid. We all do. But we
mustn't lose hope. I believe that there's a reason for
every fear we face and every hardship we suffer—and
it's to make us all stronger people."

—*Elizabeth Thatcher*

*T*imes were difficult for the widows of Coal Valley. They were still grieving the loss of their husbands and sons in the coal mine accident. All the responsibilities of life now fell on their shoulders, and the load was heavy. But then another lace-up boot dropped.

The widows discovered "Notice to Quit Premises" nailed to the doors of their company houses. Abigail Stanton and the others understood the company needed to make room for new miners who could clear the mine and rebuild, but how were the women going to move their families in two weeks' time, and where would they go? Coal Valley was their home.

With no time or money to hire a lawyer, Elizabeth Thatcher and her students searched for a legal way for the women to keep their homes, but their efforts fell short. Some of the widows wanted to give up and move on. Others wanted to fight to keep what they had. They loved their community and didn't want to lose the only homes their children had ever known. But Abigail had another idea: What if the women went to work clearing the shafts themselves?

Mayor Henry Gowen, head of the mine company, laughed when the women showed up dressed and ready to dig out the mine. They were willing to face the risks on one condition: If they could clear the shafts in time, they would have the right to stay in their homes. Mayor Gowen decided to humor them and agreed to the plan, but he fully expected them to fail within a week. He would get some work out of these stubborn women … and then still take their homes.

Can you imagine the fear and trepidation of going to work

in a collapsed coal mine? Can you picture facing the dangers of a methane gas leak, or breathing in that black dust, or banging your hands, knuckles, elbows, and knees on all those sharp rocks?

What is *your* collapsed coal mine? What eviction notices have been tacked up on your door? What situation right now feels so overwhelming that you don't think you can get through it?

In times like these, we have a few choices. We can wallow in our hardships, and become worrywarts and victims of our circumstances. Or we can do what the widows of Coal Valley did. First, they kept their eyes on the prize. Failure was not an option. Second, they had to face their fears and get outside their comfort zones—that's the only way impossible challenges become possible.

And third, they realized that they were much stronger if they labored together than they would be as individuals—because as the Scriptures tell us, a cord of many strands is an unbreakable force.

Prayer from the Heart

Father, why do I always try to fix my own problems? Why do I make a mess of things when I should just turn to you first? Please help me to trust you more in situations where I feel as if I'm trapped in a corner with no idea how to escape. Help me to get out of your way so that you can take charge. Teach me what you want me to learn from each situation, and provide the strength I need. Help me to also be vulnerable enough to ask my friends and loved ones for help. And, in turn, help me to be available when life has them in a bind. Thank you for never failing me.

❦

What's on Your Heart Today?

- How can you help to lighten the burden for others as they go through difficult times?

- How can you be more transparent with God and others when you face hardships?

- How does it change everything when you realize that God's resources and abilities are limitless?

3

But you, LORD, are a compassionate and gracious God,
slow to anger, abounding in love and faithfulness.

PSALM 86:15

"The light of love restores every lost voice."
—*Elizabeth Thatcher*

Molly Sullivan's daughter, Rosaleen, had always been a happy child, but when her father died in the mine disaster, a light in her went out like a lantern flame on a windy day.

She'd been her daddy's girl, finding delight in delivering his lunch pail to him each day at the mine. But the day he died, she entered a world of silence, almost as if her voice had died that day too.

Molly turned to Elizabeth Thatcher, hoping the town's new teacher would have some answers. Elizabeth spent extra time with Rosaleen, trying to draw her out, but nothing worked. And then, when the child went missing, everyone was frantic. A desperate search ensued with the townspeople looking everywhere. Elizabeth headed to the schoolhouse to see if Rosaleen had taken refuge there. She hadn't.

But then came a crystal clear moment for Elizabeth: She stopped to pray, asking God for guidance in finding Rosaleen. The answer to that prayer came when Elizabeth spotted a drawing the little girl had drawn of herself at the mine entrance holding a lunch pail for her father.

Elizabeth headed there quickly and made her way into the treacherous mine, calling out Rosaleen's name. And then she heard the faint sound of a child weeping. In the darkness of the mine—the place where Rosaleen's personal darkness had begun—she spilled her story. On the day of the disaster, she had chosen to play with her friend instead of taking lunch to her father. And then she heard the mountain caving in. The guilt and worry about what her mother would say when she found out Rosaleen hadn't delivered her daddy's lunch pail had overwhelmed the little girl into silence.

Guilt is powerful, isn't it? It can take root in our hearts and souls, growing with a force that overwhelms us. It's a thief that steals our joy, ruins our relationships, and comes between us and God.

The answer to Rosaleen finding her voice again began with a confession of her mistake—huge in her own mind—when she finally broke down and shared her burden, expecting shame and punishment.

But instead she received love.

Love from the teacher who cared about her deeply. Love from the mother who welcomed her back, who understood she had made an innocent mistake. And limitless love from a God who always has compassion and mercy on His children.

What guilt are you struggling with today? Has that turned your world dark and lonely? This would be the perfect time to pray and take that burden to the One with limitless grace and forgiveness. You'll discover the light of God's love is waiting there for you.

Prayer from the Heart

Father, I've carried this load of guilt for way too long. It's stolen my voice of praise and joy. It's taken over my life so much that I have trouble functioning some days. I know that your forgiveness is waiting for me, but sometimes I don't feel worthy of that. Knowing that I've hurt those I love by my actions is a heavy weight, and I don't see how they can forgive me. I know that I can't fix things without your help and guidance. Show me how I can make restitution for what I've done. Help me to leave my burden with you this time and to also learn to forgive myself. Thank you for mercy and for loving me without limits. Amen.

What's on Your Heart Today?

- What are some of the ways that guilt can affect you?

- How does prayer make a difference?

- How does God respond when you come to Him with your guilt?

4

A Whale of a Problem

Do not let those gloat over me
who are my enemies without cause;
do not let those who hate me without reason
maliciously wink the eye.
They do not speak peaceably, but devise false accusations
against those who live quietly in the land.

PSALM 35:19–20

"As a teacher, I'm drawn to the truth. Numbers don't lie and
facts are indeed facts, but sometimes we need to trust each
other, because the truth isn't always what it appears to be.
Sometimes an oil can found in a fire is not what it seems to
be. And sometimes love comes just in time to save your life."

—*Elizabeth Thatcher*

13

*N*obody in town suspected arson when flames destroyed their church. But suspicions arose when Mountie Jack Thornton discovered a blackened container of whale oil in the debris. He made it his mission to track down the guilty party.

Whale oil had to be special-ordered, so Jack was surprised to discover containers in Catherine Montgomery's shed. She said she used it for candle-making and vowed she didn't set the fire.

But other signs were pointing to Cat, especially since she was not home the night of the fire. Jack questioned her children. Her oldest, Gabe, said he didn't know where she was that evening—but she wasn't an arsonist. The youngest, Emily, spilled the news that Cat didn't arrive home until the next morning.

Later, when a necklace was found that also traced back to Cat, it seemed as if the evidence was overwhelmingly against her. Convinced that she was hiding something, Jack took Cat to his office to question her, and decided he had to lock her in a cell while he went to check out her story.

Have you ever been falsely accused of something you didn't do? The crazy thing is that these kinds of accusations don't have to be tied to big, dramatic events like an arson fire, or land you in a jail cell to bring conflict into your life. Most of the time, these situations are between a husband and wife, or a parent and a child, or a boss and an employee ... and over almost nothing. Yet they can ruin relationships and cause a lot of unnecessary anxiety.

Who do you turn to when you've been charged with something you didn't do? King David, beset upon by both enemies and people who didn't trust him, cried out to Jehovah to rescue him. Do you cry out to your Maker when life treats you unfairly? The gospel writer, James, also wrote that "the effective, fervent prayer of a righteous person avails much" (James 5:16 NKJV).

In Coal Valley, the truth about the burned church was finally revealed, and as it turned out, Cat was being framed by a jealous Pinkerton guard because she spurned his romantic advances. She had friends who stuck up for her because there is always more to the story when a light is shined on misunderstandings, or even on the secrets and lies people sometimes tell.

In your situation, God will always be your protector if you bring your needs to Him. And then do another smart thing: don't be afraid to trust a friend to have your back. Sometimes that's how God answers our prayers. He sends someone into our lives to be His hands and feet of protection over us.

Prayer from the Heart

Father, so often I mean to do well, but then I end up doing the wrong thing. Instead of trusting you with my circumstances, I try to take things into my own hands and to fix them myself. We both know that usually doesn't turn out well. Help me to trust you and to place my circumstances into your always capable hands. Thank you for the people who love me and are willing to have my back. And help me to be that kind of person for others. Remind me that things aren't always as they appear to be. Help me to dispense grace—even when it isn't warranted—and to show your love in every situation. Amen.

~~~

What's on Your Heart Today?

- If you've ever been falsely accused of doing something you didn't do, what were the events that led up to that misunderstanding?

- How did you cope with the injustice of being wrongly accused?

- How does God's protection and unlimited grace give you peace?

5

LIFE GOES ON

Weeping may endure for a night,
but joy *comes* in the morning.

PSALM 30:5B NKJV

"The more I get to know these women, I realize
how remarkable and courageous they are. They go
through life with such grace under fire. It makes me
realize just how little I know about the real world.
These women are teaching me by their example."

—*Elizabeth Thatcher*

*M*ary Dunbar embarrassed herself at Yost's Mercantile by knocking over a display of cans. One of the new miners, Dewitt Graves, helped her clean up the mess. When the grocer told Mary her tab was full, Dewitt offered to pay for her purchases.

News of that chivalry spread quickly through town. One woman made a snide remark to Abigail Stanton about Mary forgetting her late husband who had died in the mine. Abigail said, "I will never forget my Noah. But at some point, life goes on."

When Mary later bumped into Dewitt in town, she thanked him again for his kindness. He gave her a wink and hinted that he hadn't had a home-cooked meal in quite some time, which made her smile.

The next night, Mary's son, Caleb, wasn't happy that Dewitt was sitting at their table—the place where his father once sat—or that he had asked Mary to the Miner's Dance.

After school one day, the boy really struggled about his mom starting a relationship with Dewitt, so Elizabeth asked Caleb to share a memory of his father with her. The words flooded from him. His pa was strong and tall. He liked to sing and whistle and take Caleb fishing. He missed him so much and *nobody* could take his place.

On the night of the dance, as Dewitt left with Mary, Caleb wept. And then he got an idea. He dug through an old storage trunk, finding his father's suit coat, inhaling the scent of his pa that still clung faintly.

Not much later, as music filled the room at the dance and

smiling townsfolks did the two-step and waltzed, Caleb walked in wearing his pa's big coat. When Mary saw him, her eyes glistened with tears. And then Caleb did something amazing. He cut in, asking his mother for a dance as the entire town watched.

Moving on with our lives after a painful loss is always agonizing, isn't it? Have you experienced the loss of a loved one like Caleb did, or the loss of a job or a friendship? Perhaps you have a prodigal child you're grieving. Or you've had a serious health crisis yourself. Well, guess what? The last time we checked, the mortality rate among human beings is 100 percent. Loss is an equal opportunist.

But God has a plan for us in every situation. And it's a great plan. He wants us to prosper and He wants us to have a hope and a future. That doesn't mean life will ever be pain-free, but just as Mary and Caleb learned to cope with their loss with "grace under fire," as Elizabeth put it, so can we.

Prayer from the Heart

Father, it's hard to move forward after difficult circumstances or the loss of a loved one. I've often allowed myself to become stuck in sadness and despair, to wallow in self-pity or pain when I've experienced moments like these that have broken my heart. Even worse, I've sometimes been angry at you and allowed bitterness to fill my soul. Remind me to come to you for comfort. Change is hard, but help me to move forward so that I can serve you. You never waste any of our tears, so please help me not to waste them either. Help me to pick up the broken pieces of my life, to take what I've learned, and to use those moments for your glory. Amen.

What's on Your Heart Today?

- Why is it so hard to move on after your heart has been broken?

- How can you respond to those moments with grace under fire?

- How can you use what you've learned from those hard places?

6

LOVE IS TRICKY

There are three things that are too amazing for me,
four that I do not understand:
the way of an eagle in the sky,
the way of a snake on a rock,
the way of a ship on the high seas,
and the way of a man with a young woman.

PROVERBS 30:18–19

"Why are relationships between men and women
sometimes so confusing? Our actions. Our words.
It's like we're all speaking in foreign tongues
and we can't understand each other."

—*Elizabeth Thatcher*

*I*t didn't take long for new miner Billy Hamilton to notice Elizabeth Thatcher. You can imagine how well received that was by Jack Thornton. But there was more to it than jealousy. He had a gut feeling something wasn't right, and when he received a tip that Billy wasn't who he said he was, Jack relayed it to Elizabeth. But she was annoyed. Billy was charming and he truly seemed to want to court her. Besides, what right did Jack have to interfere, given he was slow as a country mule in the relationship department?

As evidence piled up against Billy, Jack tried several times to warn Elizabeth, but he just kept digging himself in a deeper hole. Meanwhile, Billy was attentive and even poetic with her. He admitted she was the type of woman he could settle down with. And it seemed Billy could read her like a book, even having insights about her family back home.

In fact, a little too much insight. Elizabeth realized she'd never mentioned her family to Billy. Leery now that he might be a carpetbagger, she decided to make up a story to flush out his true intentions. She told Billy that her father had disinherited her because he was so upset about her leaving home. Billy didn't seem cowed by this, but she was growing suspicious.

Not much later, as Billy tried to bolt out of town on a stolen horse, Jack was waiting. He dragged Billy from the horse and locked him up. Elizabeth was devastated that she'd almost made a big misstep with Billy. In her private wish that Jack would declare his own feelings for her, she had fallen for a different type of hope in another man, and it fluttered away.

Relationships can be tricky, can't they? Whether with our

spouses or potential spouses, or even with friendships. The last time we checked, all 7.45 billion people on Earth have free will. That's a lot of folks running around with their own self-centered agendas. It's a wonder any of us ever find that one, true soulmate. Which means it's even more important to seek God's wisdom for good relationship decisions. We need to spend time in prayer, studying the Scriptures, and holding out for someone who shares our faith. The Bible tells us not to be yoked together with unbelievers, because "what fellowship can light have with darkness?" (2 Corinthians 6:14).

And one more tip. Listen to those who love you and have your best interests at heart. Sometimes when our judgments are blinded, a trusted loved one or friend with x-ray relationship vision can save us from making mistakes that will haunt us for the rest of our lives.

Prayer from the Heart

Father, I realize that having my heart set on the wrong person can greatly impact my life. Help me to make wise decisions when it comes to those I allow into my inner circle. Give me good discernment, and help me to carefully choose those with whom I will be transparent and vulnerable. Help me to be that same kind of trustworthy person for those who bring me into their inner circle. I know that matters of the heart are some of the most confusing and important decisions I will ever make in my life. Help me to choose well. Remind me to spend time with you, because I know that's where true wisdom will always be revealed, no matter what decision I have to make.

What's on Your Heart Today?

· Why are relationship decisions sometimes so confusing?

· What have you learned from past decisions in relationships, either good or bad?

· How can you make wise decisions about future relationships?

7

IF YOU BAKE IT, THEY WILL COME

"See, I am doing a new thing!
Now it springs up; do you not perceive it?
I am making a way in the wilderness
and streams in the wasteland."

ISAIAH 43:19

"Before I came here, I thought my purpose was teaching
at one of those big city schools. God shut that door and
He opened up another one—a much more meaningful
one. And that is teaching here in Coal Valley. And I just
know God will show you what He wants for you too."

—Elizabeth Thatcher

*E*lizabeth Thatcher sampled some of Abigail Stanton's baked goods one morning and was stunned. She told Abigail her family had employed some of Hamilton's finest chefs and their scones couldn't hold a candle to hers. Abigail was taken aback and the compliment awakened a dream she'd kept hidden.

Gathering her courage, Abigail met with Mayor Henry Gowen to ask about reopening the old café he owned. Ever the shark, Mayor Gowen said she could reopen the cafe, but she'd have to split the profits with him. She would also have to deed her row house to him.

Abigail had already lost so much ... her husband ... her son ... life as she knew it. As she ran her hands over the notches on the doorframe that she had used to measure her son's growth, she wondered how she could give up a home filled with so many memories. She was no longer a wife. No longer a mother. What was her purpose now?

Abigail entered the old café. Fears hovered as she stood there considering the junk on the floor, the cobwebs, the leaky roof. They were an ironic picture of her life now.

When nightfall hit and Abigail hadn't come home, Elizabeth became worried. Jack Thornton thought he knew where she might be and took Elizabeth to the old café, where they found Abigail asleep, worn out from cleaning the place. She told Elizabeth that she'd kept her fixer-upper project a secret so folks wouldn't think she was crazy.

The next day, she signed the deal with Mayor Gowen to open the café, and then started baking. Miles Montgomery poked his head in the door, having smelled her cookies, and asked if he could buy some. He said, "I sure hope you have more—because you're going to need 'em." When she walked outside, she found townsfolk lined down the street and around the corner.

What dream or goal have you been afraid to pursue? Sometimes life's changes put us into purpose limbo. When the children of Israel were wandering in the desert for forty years, they returned to a brook that had once given them water, but the brook had dried up. They were depressed. Life wasn't fair. Do you know what they had to do? They had to go find a new brook.

Sometimes the only way we can find a new purpose, or reach a new blessing God has in store for us, is to be willing to turn loose of things that are precious to us and take a step outside our comfort zone. It's a scary step. But as Abigail discovered, others can't enjoy our cookies and scones until we get them out there.

Prayer from the Heart

Lord, sometimes I'm angry at you when my plans fall apart, because I don't understand why. Help me to trust you even when I don't understand. I know that your purposes for me are always better than anything I could ever plan for myself. Give me the courage to step out in faith to accomplish the tasks you have for me. Thank you for loving me too much to give me everything I request. Help me to ask for the right things, and to turn loose of the past so I can move forward to the future you've planned for me. Thank you for being with me whenever I leave my comfort zone, and for going ahead of me to prepare the way.

What's on Your Heart Today?

- Why does God sometimes block the plans we've made?

- Why is it such a struggle to step out in faith?

- How do you respond when God has a different purpose for you than what you planned?

8

YOU ARE MORE THAN ENOUGH

Consider it pure joy, my brothers and sisters,
whenever you face trials of many kinds.

JAMES 1:2

"If there is one thing I've learned about the people
of this town it's that they don't quit, even when everything is against them. So, we are not going to quit."

—*Elizabeth Thatcher*

A large gathering stood waiting for the stagecoach to arrive with one of the few survivors of the town's mining disaster. The mine collapse had killed forty-seven men, leaving dozens of fatherless children and many, many widows—virtually all but one. Adam Miller was in the hospital for months, and his wife and two daughters were eager to see him again. The rest of the town was equally excited. His arrival home would be a seed of hope for everyone.

But none of them anticipated that when Adam stepped off that stagecoach, he would do so with only one good leg and a crude wooden peg leg. Their cheers fell quickly to uncomfortable silence. Mrs. Miller pushed her daughters toward him and they all awkwardly embraced. They were happy that Adam was alive, but stunned at his appearance.

Eager to prove he wasn't just half a man, Adam jumped back into his job at the coal mine but quickly found it impossible. Not only was he permanently disabled, he was suffering post-traumatic stress disorder. Every time the mine whistle blew, he would relive the accident. Finally, in despair, he quit. Even at home, he felt like a puzzle piece that no longer fit. When his wife and girls presented Adam with a new prosthetic leg, paid for by a town fund-raiser, he went into a rage, feeling he had been turned into a charity case. Not knowing how to provide any longer, he rode off into the wilderness, convinced his family would be better off without him.

Fortunately, Mountie Jack Thornton tracked him down and was able to talk him into coming back home by proving that he was worth much more to the world than the sum of his able body parts.

Things don't always turn out the way we plan, do they? When life hits us with disaster, it's common to have feelings of worthlessness like Adam did. But your worth doesn't come from having a whole body or the perfect job. It comes from your Maker. You are worthy because God made you. You are His masterpiece.

Sometimes our biggest obstacles are inside our own heads.

Are you struggling with low self-worth? Well, guess what? You have infinite worth because you are a child of a king. The King of kings. The world would have you believe your value comes from your appearance, your job, your house, or your net worth. Don't believe that for a second. If you are feeling less than, take some time to review the promises of Scripture about just how valuable you are to God. Then do as Adam did, come home again. You *are* enough. In fact, more than enough … because God says so.

Prayer from the Heart

God, thank you for creating me. On days when I feel less than adequate, remind me that I am fearfully and wonderfully made. I am enough, Lord, because I was made in your image, which makes me infinitely valuable. It's so easy to compare myself to others and feel like I don't measure up. Help me to know my worth is in you alone. Give me the strength to control my thoughts about myself. Just as I wouldn't normally talk rudely to, or about someone else, help me not to speak ugly words about myself either. Show me who I am in you, and help me to be all that you created me to be. Thank you for loving me just as I am.

⁂

What's on Your Heart Today?

· In what area of your life do you feel less than adequate?

· What are some strengths that God has placed in you?

· How can you use those strengths to overcome the areas where you feel inadequate?

9

CLEAR AS MUD

Many are the plans in the mind of a man,
but it is the purpose of the LORD that will stand.

PROVERBS 19:21 ESV

**"Sometimes you see a girl and
your whole future is clear as a bell."**

—Gabe Montgomery

When Jack Thornton first arrived in Coal Valley, he hadn't been happy with his posting. He and Elizabeth Thatcher had gotten off to an icy start, so he put in for a transfer. But that had been long ago. Since then, things had warmed between them and he had forgotten all about his request. Until a communique arrived from headquarters—a letter of reassignment. Now he had a tough decision to make. Refusing the transfer could stall his career. But worse, he dreaded telling Elizabeth.

Jack had once told her that he could never marry because it wouldn't be fair to a young lady to put her through a life as a Mountie's wife. But now, as he invited her for Saturday night supper (to her delight), he clarified his position. "Please consider this an act of courtship."

Jack arranged for a private dinner at Abigail's Café. Dozens of candles lit the room. Romance filled the air as the food was served, and they danced to music from a Victrola. For Elizabeth, the night could not have been more enchanting. But Jack knew he had to share his difficult news with her.

The following day, he took Elizabeth to his favorite overlook and then dropped the bombshell about the new posting. Elizabeth was devastated, but Jack told her that his heart was now in Coal Valley, and he would be appealing the transfer. However, Elizabeth cried that she couldn't let him do that. She could never jeopardize his career.

A love story that was so clear to both of them only the night before was now very muddy.

Isn't it crazy how good plans can get messed up so fast?

Have you ever experienced that? We ask God to do His will in our lives—but how do we know what that is? And what should we do when there are two choices and no clear path as to which one is better?

That's the time to get on our knees and ask God to show us which choice is just a good thing and which is a "God-thing." You see, God has already revealed much of His plan for us in His guidebook for life—the Bible. If we truly follow His teachings, spend time in prayer, and seek wise counsel from those we trust, we're already doing God's will.

Years later with the beauty of hindsight, Jack and Elizabeth were able to look back and see how God worked out all the details when they stepped out in faith regarding Jack's transfer issue. And in all the important decisions facing us—we can be confident of His will for us too.

Prayer from the Heart

Lord, sometimes I worry about my future as it stretches before me with numerous twists and turns. My heart's desire is to do what you want for my life. Go before me and make the path clear. Give me peace about my decisions. Place big warning signs ahead of me when I'm moving away from your plans. Please take away my selfish desires and replace them with what you want. Help me to have more good days than bad days following your will for me. Give me a willing spirit and remind me that I don't travel this journey alone. I trust that you've gone ahead of me and you've already prepared the road that I should take.

What's on Your Heart Today?

- How should you respond when your future is unclear and you don't know what to do?

- Do you ever feel afraid of God's will for you? How do you conquer that fear?

- Think about a time when you stepped out in faith toward a future goal. What did you learn?

🍂 *10* 🍂

REGRET ME NOT

"For where your treasure is,
there your heart will be also."

MATTHEW 6:21 NKJV

"I was at your father's funeral, and I remember
thinking he was a truly rich man. He got a good
woman and a fine son to weep over him and
remember him. That's true wealth. I only hope
when I draw my last breath, there's someone
there to feel that way about me."

—*Constable Sam Collins*

Jack Thornton hated being away from Elizabeth Thatcher. But his assignment was a noble one as he scoured the countryside for the notorious Tolliver Gang.

In Coal Valley, Elizabeth's sister, Julie, cared for Nathaniel, the wounded man she'd stumbled upon in the forest. When Julie finally told Elizabeth about Nate and his outlaw past, Elizabeth fretted that her sister had put the whole town in danger.

Meanwhile, Jack encountered a patrol of Mounties who told him they had spotted Nate Tolliver's horse near Coal Valley and they believed the gang was hiding nearby. Jack galloped off at a furious pace. Everything he treasured was there.

What he didn't know was that the gang was already riding into town searching for their leader who had gone missing from their forest cabin hideout. When they tracked him to the café, they bound and gagged Abigail Stanton and took Elizabeth and Julie hostage (bargaining chips) and moved them to their cabin. There, while Nate continued recuperating, they dug up the stolen treasure they had buried earlier.

When Jack arrived back in town and found Abigail, and heard the whole story, he realized he had to act, but was seriously outmanned. With an ingenious bluff involving red tablecloths perched on horses that were tied off in the trees (to make the gang think they were surrounded), Jack was able to take down Nate Tolliver and his gang, and rescue the women.

Julie was mortified that her naiveté at being duped by a handsome outlaw had almost gotten her and Elizabeth injured;

or worse, put Jack in harm's way. She had a bundle of remorse that would haunt her for a long time.

When Constable Sam Collins arrived a few days later to escort the gang to trial, Jack learned this would be the retiring officer's last mission. Jack asked him if he had any regrets about choosing the Mountie life. The constable said he had just one—not taking more time for family.

Regrets get in the way of life, don't they? The mistakes of youth, the sins of commission, like choosing a relationship for the wrong reasons, can immobilize us with shame for a long time. Likewise, so can mistakes of omission, like being focused on the wrong kind of treasure.

When we reach the end of our lives, none of us will wish we'd spent more time at the office or worked eighty hours a week to get rich. Instead, we'll wish we'd had more time with our families and done more for God and others. The decisions we make each day will determine if we'll reach the end of our days with a bitter or better treasure. Better is always better.

Prayer from the Heart

Father, there are so many choices in my life and so many responsibilities that demand my attention. Sometimes, even though I think my heart is in the right place, I make the mistake of moving ahead without asking for your guidance first. I get impatient and make snap decisions that get me in trouble. Help me to wait on you and to keep my eyes on what's truly important. Remind me to keep you first in my life. Show me that the years with my family, loved ones, and friends will zoom by, and that I can't go back and rewind those days. They are my treasure. Don't let me forget where true wealth is found, and thank you for blessing me with such abundance.

What's on Your Heart Today?

- How have your impulses or choices led to regrets?

- What are your treasures—your true wealth?

- How can you keep from messing up when it comes to the most important choices?

11

PROCEED WITH CAUTION

For in the day of trouble
he will keep me safe in his dwelling;
he will hide me in the shelter of his sacred tent
and set me high upon a rock.

PSALM 27:5

**"I think it is safer in here with you
than out there, Buddy."**

—*Jack Thornton*

When Constable Jack Thornton rode back into town after rounding up the Nate Tolliver gang, he had one thing on his mind—Elizabeth Thatcher. As his horse rounded the corner onto Main Street, that's just who he saw. Her beauty took his breath away, and when she caught sight of him, her face lit up—which made him smile, until the woman Elizabeth was speaking with turned around. It was Rosemary Leveaux. Jack's ex-fiancé.

Just when things were going so well between him and Elizabeth, Rosemary swooped into town to steal the show, like the actress she was. While Jack cautioned her that things were over between them, Rosemary wasn't one to be snubbed. Even though it had been two years since she broke up with him, she imagined picking back up right where they left off, determined to convince him of the same.

But Jack had his heart set on Elizabeth now, and he had to make both ladies understand that he no longer had feelings for Rosemary. Which was proving to be tougher than he thought. The whole town was caught up in Whirlwind Rosemary. Men swooned as she walked past, ladies all wanted to wear her signature color of red, and every time Jack tried to find time alone with Elizabeth to explain, Rosemary appeared and ratcheted up the dilemma.

Perhaps you can relate to Jack. Have you ever found yourself in a sticky misunderstanding with someone where it seemed no matter how hard you tried to explain, you just kept digging yourself into a deeper hole with them? Or they were just so hard-headed you couldn't get a word in edgewise? So much so that you wanted to lock yourself away with a dog or some other nonhuman because you knew at least they wouldn't misread anything you'd say?

In the same way, God will never misconstrue you. He knows your heart, your motives. Back before God laid the foundations of the world in place, He knew what you were going to say at any given moment of your life. He is your shelter in the storms of your circumstances and a refuge of understanding in the sea of chaotic relationships.

When you feel no one gets you, when no one will take the time to really listen to you, just tell God what's on your heart. He will listen; He will comfort you; He will give you peace about your situation. And one more thing: That annoying human in your life who keeps being obtuse with you? Give that dilemma to God, and give it time. Somewhere, sometime, everybody always ends up eating a slice of humble pie. Even the Rosemary Leveauxs in your life.

Prayer from the Heart

Father, life tends to get messy for me sometimes. And when it does, I often foolishly try to sort things out on my own. It seems the harder I try, the worse I mess things up. Please help me, Lord. Help me not to depend on myself, but to run to you. Bring light to the circumstances in my life, and allow truth to be made known. Help me to discern the truth from the lies the world would have me believe. Let your truth shine through me, and to me. Bless my relationships and help me to honor you in them. When trials come, draw me close to you and shelter me from the storm. Thank you for letting me find refuge in you.

What's on Your Heart Today?

- What is a sticky situation you have tried to solve on your own?

- What are the truths of the circumstances you're dealing with in your situation?

- How can you allow those truths to be made known so they will help to foster a resolution?

$\mathscr{C}\!\!\mathscr{E}$ *12* $\mathscr{D}\!\!\mathscr{D}$

LARGE AND IN CHARGE

There is a time for everything,
and a season for every activity under the heavens:
a time to be born and a time to die,
a time to plant and a time to uproot,
a time to kill and a time to heal,
a time to tear down and a time to build,
a time to weep and a time to laugh,
a time to mourn and a time to dance.

ECCLESIASTES 3:1–4

"For what is life but a bittersweet mix of sadness,
wonderment, hope, and joy?"
—*Elizabeth Thatcher*

*T*he citizens of Coal Valley all seemed to have their noses out of joint. That was *never* a good thing. Since the church had burned down weeks before, Sunday services were being held in the woods and school classes in the saloon, which had become sort of a "schaloon." Mountie Bill Avery was elbow-deep into an investigation of the mine accident and had ruffled the feathers of Mayor Henry Gowen, who appeared to be hiding something about the mine explosion. When there is smoke, there is usually fire, right? To top it off, Rosemary Leveaux was still in full pursuit of Jack Thornton, and Elizabeth Thatcher was as confused as ever.

When Abigail Stanton continued pressing for answers about the mine collapse that had killed her husband, Noah, and forty-six other brave fathers and husbands, Mayor Gowen claimed to have new evidence. He brought in his own lawyer, and then in a heart-wrenching moment for Abigail, he laid the fault for the mine disaster directly at the feet of Noah Stanton. He said Noah knew of the unsafe conditions of the mine, but covered it up and sent the men into the mine anyway—including his and Abigail's own son—because he was deep in debt and needed money. Abigail wondered how she'd ever prove that Mayor Gowen's words weren't true.

Even Elizabeth was struggling with her own decisions about the future. Her father, concerned for her safety, had told her in a letter that he had found her a teaching position at a prestigious school back home. Only days before, Elizabeth wouldn't have given the letter a second thought, but

Rosemary's presence and not knowing Jack's true feelings had made her think strongly about leaving Coal Valley.

The whole town seemed to be on the verge of another explosion.

How do you handle the uncertainties in your life? Did you know the Bible says that God has allowed a season for *everything* in our time on this earth? Yes, even for the painful things there is a season: for hardship, injustice, grief, and death. Even confusion. But He has also promised that there will be a season for justice, fresh starts, clarity, and best of all, hope.

Are you experiencing unrest like the folks of Coal Valley? Hang on to the promise that there is a time for everything. And know that God is holy, wise, powerful, loving, and good. Try to give Him praise in all your circumstances, and He will carry you in His strong arms all the days of your life. In other words, He is large and in charge, and bigger than any problem you could ever have.

Prayer from the Heart

Father, I know your Word says there is a time for everything. But when I am going through hardships and uncertainty, it's challenging to remember you have promised to be with me in difficult times and in good. Help me to see your hand in every situation. Let me look for joy and find reasons to be thankful in all things. Let your joy shine so brightly in me that others take notice and recognize it as you, living *in* me. Thank you for every blessing in my life. And thank you that your blessings are always just around the corner. I praise you for producing rainbows after the storms in my life.

ᘓᓍᘐᓎ

What's on Your Heart Today?

- What are some areas of unrest or uncertainty in your life right now?

- How can you see God's hand in every situation— even the tough ones?

- What are some times where you've seen good things come out of bad situations?

∞ *13* ∞

THE CURE FOR EVERYTHING

Be anxious for nothing, but in everything
by prayer and supplication, with thanksgiving,
let your requests be made known to God.

PHILIPPIANS 4:6 NKJV

"I've always found that the best way
to wash away worry is through prayer."
—*Molly Sullivan*

A group of townspeople waited for the stagecoach to arrive. Jaws dropped as the prosecutor got off the stage and they realized that Sam Madison was actually *Samantha* Madison. She assured them she had been to law school, but this just increased their worries about the pending trial. Sam soon realized she had a big challenge ahead. In addition to Mayor Henry Gowen's lies and Judge Parker's apparent fraternizing with their opposition, she only had forty-eight hours to be ready for court.

Abigail Stanton had so much at stake—not just convicting those who'd been negligent in the mine disaster, but restoring her late husband Noah's reputation.

Sam was relieved when she found Joseph Sweeney, an auditor from the Bureau of Mines, who was willing to testify for them. He said that Abigail's husband and son were innocent. Noah had contacted him about unsafe conditions in the mine. Joseph had found that the ventilation system wasn't working properly and recommended that operations be suspended. Mayor Gowen's report said something different, but Joseph swore that it was a forgery. The worrisome part was that their case depended entirely on him.

Sam made her opening statement as the trial began. She said she would prove that the Pacific Northwest Mining Company knew conditions were unsafe, but they had left the men in the mine anyway. But when she called Joseph to the stand, he changed his testimony. He said the ventilation system was safe and the company was not at fault. The defense attorney then quickly turned the tables on Sam, claiming that the catastrophe was a clear case of negligence by Noah Stanton. The entire courtroom was stunned, nobody more than Abigail. If she thought she had worries before, how would she ever prove Noah's innocence now?

What tables have been turned on you and what are you worried about these days? God's Word has a lot to say on the topic. It counsels us not to be anxious about anything—what clothes to wear, what food to eat, or even what to say at any given moment in time. And yet, we all know worry is like dry rot to our souls and our connection to God. It can defeat us, make us sick, and ruin our relationships. And it doesn't accomplish a thing except to make God seem far away. Well, if that's how you feel … guess who moved?

The antidote for worry is to take action: *Turn it over to God!* And then sit back and relax. He's got it, and He doesn't need your advice on what to do next. Your trust is all He's looking for, and it will melt your worry into contentment and peace.

Prayer from the Heart

Lord, I know I worry too much. I see things I can't fix and situations where loved ones are hurting, and I don't know how to make things better. That bothers me so much that I often feel like I can't even breathe. Help me to pray about things more than I whine about them. Sometimes I forget that you're my *Father*, and that I am your beloved child. When I bring my worries and burdens to you, help me to leave them there rather than picking them up and starting the worry process all over again like I usually do. Thank you for being a prayer-answering God. I'm grateful that none of my concerns are trivial matters to you.

꙰

What's on Your Heart Today?

- Why do you think people worry so much?

- Why do we bring our worries to God and then pick them up again?

- Why do we sometimes talk about our worries so often … and pray about them so little?

14

IF THE LACE-UP BOOT FITS

If any of you lacks wisdom, you should ask God,
who gives generously to all without finding fault,
and it will be given to you.

JAMES 1:5

"Sometimes we spend so much time searching
for the answers, we don't realize
they are right under our nose."
—*Charles Kensington*

*E*lizabeth Thatcher had a foot in two worlds. One foot was squarely planted in the small town of Hope Valley, which had newly been renamed, since "Coal Valley" didn't fit a town that no longer mined coal, and since hope seemed to be its most important feature to go along with its outhouses and simple virtues. Elizabeth's other foot slid quite nicely into society life back home in Hamilton, with servants, afternoon tea, and fancy ball gowns. One was everything she had known her whole life. In the other, everything was new—life on the frontier, independence, and a man who made her stomach flutter.

When Elizabeth got news her mother was sick, she rushed home. As she nursed her back to health, her old suitor, Charles Kensington, began showing up at her house, reminding her of their past. He even pointed out where he had carved their initials on a tree at her family's estate, telling her, "Some things were meant to endure." Her family wasted no time pointing out Charles' attributes. He was kind, handsome, and had a good job.

While Elizabeth and Charles were reliving old times, Jack Thornton was back in Hope Valley, swinging a hammer. He had donated his reward money from capturing the Tolliver gang to help rebuild the church and school, and now he was spending every free moment doing the construction work himself. He even enlisted the help of the new timber tycoon, Lee Coulter. Jack's heart was in every nail he drove into the wood. He wanted to provide a classroom for the woman who had captured his heart and show her that Hope Valley was the place for her—which left Elizabeth with a hard decision. Should she stay with the safe and comfortable, or should she take a risk with her life and her love?

Choices like these are never easy. Have you ever prayed for God to make the answers to your prayers super obvious? Wouldn't it be great if God sent a sky-writer to paint His life-directions into the sky for us? Such as "Take the job" or "This is the man (or woman) for you." Well, guess what? He does ... only it's His "heart-writer." The Bible says God has sent us a helper, the Holy Spirit, to teach us everything we need to make wise decisions.

What decisions are you faced with today? Sometimes, like Elizabeth's decision, both options may seem worthy. But which is the one God has planned for you? The key is we must turn off the noise of the world along with our own inner conversations and listen. Really listen for God's heart-writer. The answers will arrive plain as day.

Prayer from the Heart

Father, I want my life to be pleasing to you, but when I'm faced with multiple paths, it's hard to know which one to take. What if I choose the wrong one? Please speak the right answers into my heart and grant me wisdom to know the best choices for me. God, clear the paths that only you can clear, and close the ones that need to be blocked. Make your will abundantly plain for my life. Show me the way that I should take. Let your light shine so brightly that I can see where the next step should be. Thank you, Lord, for your guidance and discernment. Thank you for the opportunities you give me. Let me use them to bring you glory.

What's on Your Heart Today?

- What decision are you facing today where you wish God would give you a clear answer?

- What can you do while you wait on Him?

- Which of the two paths would bring God more glory?

15

NOT THE LAST RESORT

This is the confidence we have in approaching God:
that if we ask anything according to his will,
he hears us.

1 JOHN 5:14

"You're a self-made man, Mr. Coulter,
and you should be proud of that. But no one does it
alone. We all need help at times."

—*Pastor Frank Hogan*

*A*pproval, influence, fairness, providential treatment: all of those words describe what we call "favor." We all hope to gain it with our friends, families, and employers, but Lee Coulter desperately needed it. The entrepreneur behind the new timber company in Hope Valley had done everything he knew how to do to get his business started. He'd hired the former miners and trained them. He'd set up offices on Main Street, and got all the components at the sawmill built and ready. Except for one. He couldn't get the diesel engine running—which was needed to start the saw blades churning.

Head bowed in defeat, Lee sat in the saloon. Pastor Frank Hogan came and sat in the chair next to him. He asked Lee what was troubling him. Lee shared his frustration at not being able to get the engine up and running, which was now, apparently, the lynchpin to bringing new jobs to Hope Valley and having a viable business. Pastor Frank suggested that Lee needed to ask God for favor. Lee chuckled at the suggestion: "No disrespect, Pastor, but I think the Big Guy has better things to do than to fix my mill." Lee explained that he had been in tighter jams before and he was sure *he* would figure something out. Lee was used to relying on himself when problems arose instead of calling on God.

But as Pastor Frank stood to leave, the worried Lee second-guessed himself. He told the pastor if he wanted to pray for the mill, surely it couldn't hurt.

Isn't that the way it is for us too? When problems arise, we rely on ourselves first, and then turn to God as a last resort.

Pastor Frank smiled as he walked away, knowing Lee had

sort of backed into two of the most important words: "Help me." Imagine Lee's surprise the next day when a man walked into the saloon shaking off the rain, telling Lee and Mountie Jack Thornton the storms were so bad they had forced him to detour through Hope Valley. When they asked where he was headed, he told them he was supposed to fix an engine at the textile factory in Buxton. It just so happened that this man, who God had rerouted right into the saloon, was in fact a diesel mechanic.

Scripture promises that God is a good Father, who, if we need bread, will not give us a rock instead. He sometimes doesn't answer our prayers in the way we expect, but God grants us what we need. Do you need to ask a favor from your Father today? Don't back your way into prayer. Make it your first choice.

Prayer from the Heart

Father, forgive me for thinking I can rely on myself to fix my problems instead of trusting in you first. We both know what a mess I can make of that. Help me not to use you as a last resort. Instead, let me run to you immediately when I have an issue or concern. Lord, you are capable of anything. All things are possible with you. You control the wind and the rain, and there is nothing you cannot do. Let me remember you are the ultimate problem solver and that you often fix my issues before I even ask. Thank you for all the times you have come to my rescue. May I always recognize your hand in my blessings.

✿✿✿✿

What's on Your Heart Today?

- What are some problems you've been trying to solve on your own?

- Why do you think you try every other solution first before coming to God?

- In what ways have you seen God answer your prayers?

16

LET GO OF THE TREE TRUNK

"Have I not commanded you? Be strong and
of good courage; do not be afraid, nor be dismayed,
for the LORD your God *is* with you wherever you go."

JOSHUA 1:9 NKJV

"From the time we're young, people assume
we're not capable of certain things.
Sometimes we just need to prove 'em wrong."

—*Jack Thornton*

*E*lizabeth Thatcher overheard Mr. Harper in the mercantile. As a widower, he was in a bind. He'd hoped Florence Blakeley could help care for his children while he was away. She couldn't, but Elizabeth raised her hand. She'd been brought up with wealth and privilege, a woman who, when she first arrived in town, spent an uncomfortable few days before braving the outhouse. So you could forgive Mr. Harper for being doubtful about her fortitude. When he hinted that Jack Thornton should check on her, Elizabeth said she was perfectly capable of taking care of the kids without anyone's help.

But when she arrived at his rough-hewn cabin, she wasn't quite so confident. Mr. Harper gave her a list of instructions. Elizabeth was taken aback at having to milk the cow and start a fire at 4:00 in the morning, and about needing to lock the door to keep the coyotes out. The thought of coyotes in the cabin definitely got her attention.

It was a rude awakening the next morning when the children stirred Elizabeth's slumber before dawn. Yes, it was time to start the chores: mucking out the stalls, collecting eggs, and more. It didn't take Elizabeth long to learn that homesteading would be a huge challenge.

Jack came to check on Elizabeth and informed her that Mr. Harper had been delayed another day. And it didn't help when the kids had to ask the name of the brown sludge Elizabeth had dished onto their supper plates. Courageous man that he was, Jack bravely offered to eat a little more of her "delicious and hearty" vegetable stew.

After an exhausted Elizabeth put the children to bed, Jack

told her he was proud of her—she had done something that was definitely beyond her normal level of comfort.

Sometimes God asks us to inch our way out to the end of the tree limb, away from the safety of the tree trunk. It's scary out there, shaky and unstable, and we often shrink from the risk. And yet out there is where God has left all the good fruit for us. Sometimes, we're cowed by self-doubt. Other times, we listen to others' doubt about us. But either way, we focus on what we *can't* do instead of trusting what God *can* do through us.

We think we are not worthy to be used by God and forget that all He's asking for is a willing heart and a little trust. Elizabeth messed up many times at the Harper ranch, but in the end, both she and the kids survived, better for the experience. What limb is God urging you onto? It's time to take a deep breath and go get that sweet fruit.

Prayer from the Heart

God, sometimes your dreams for me seem too big. I know *you're* able, but I'm not so sure about myself. Fear overwhelms me when I think about doing what you've asked me to do. That first step of faith seems like a giant step. What if I fail? What if I disappoint you? Please help me to remember that I can do all things through you. Show me the purpose you have for me, and stretch me. Give me courage. And help me to remember that I won't take that first step (or any of them) alone. I'm grateful that even though I might be out of my comfort zone, you'll never be out of yours.

⌘

What's on Your Heart Today?

- Why do you think God sometimes asks you to get outside your comfort zone?

- How can you overcome the fear that keeps you from taking the risks God is asking you to take?

- What have you learned from previous times when you've stepped out in faith?

✵ 17 ✵

TAKE NO FOR AN ANSWER

Wait for the LORD;
be strong and take heart
and wait for the LORD.

PSALM 27:14

"When you truly love someone,
all you want is for them to be happy."

—*Abigail Stanton*

Charles Kensington was used to getting what he wanted. As the best sales person for Mr. Thatcher's shipping company, he was accustomed to coming out on top, and he led a privileged life. Charles grew up in a well-to-do, big-city family, and couldn't fathom why his old teenage flame, Elizabeth Thatcher—whose upbringing was just like his—would choose a simple life in Hope Valley over a life with him in Hamilton.

Elizabeth was more than surprised when Charles showed up in her classroom one afternoon. She had never seen him outside the trappings of her home city, and she was suspicious. Charles assured her his intentions were pure—her father's company had just signed a contract with Lee Coulter for lumber to make shipping crates, but Elizabeth wasn't buying it. She knew that they could have arranged that by telegram.

Elizabeth agreed to show Charles around town, and as they walked near the picturesque pond, he reminded her that she had friends and family back home who loved and missed her. There it was … the true reason for his trip. Elizabeth then reminded him of something she had told her family on her last trip home: her calling was to the children of Hope Valley. They needed her, and her place was there with them. Charles knew there was more to it than that. He knew her heart belonged to Jack Thornton. This conversation was not over. Not by a long shot.

Have you ever wanted something so badly you worked to pry open a door that was shut? Occasionally God answers prayers by shutting a door—sometimes for our protection and sometimes just because He knows what's best for us. While we tend to place all our attention on the here and now, God sees our every need from the perspective of eternity, and how our choices and desires have ripple effects through our entire lives.

But no matter how you slice it, "no" is always hard to hear. It was hard for Charles, and it's hard for us. We can get so focused on what *we* want that we forget to ask what *God* wants. He can and will smash doors wide open for us—in His time and if it's His will. But they have to be the right doors.

Sometimes, through our own stubbornness and force of will, we smash through the wrong doors. Have you ever done that? What do you usually find on the other side? A world of hurt, right? Wrong door, wrong outcome. The key is, don't tell God what *you* want; ask Him what *He* wants. Right door, right outcome.

Prayer from the Heart

Lord, waiting is one of the hardest things to do. We live in a push-button society where we want things to happen instantaneously. Forgive me for losing patience. Help me to understand that sometimes good things take time, and that waiting builds character. God, give me patience while I wait. Open my eyes to your eternal picture. When the answer is no, help me to accept it gracefully. Draw me close to you during this period of waiting. Thank you for your never-ending patience with me. Thank you for the times your "no" has been for my protection. Help me to live with the boldness to walk through open doors and the grace to walk past the ones that are shut.

What's on Your Heart Today?

- Describe a time when you've lost patience and tried to open a door that appeared to be shut.

- What are some reasons God might shut a door?

- How can you spend your wait time drawing closer to God?

18

SPIRITUAL TOOTH DECAY

Bear with each other and forgive one another
if any of you has a grievance against someone.
Forgive as the Lord forgave you.

COLOSSIANS 3:13

"Here's my two cents about anger. It's like a toothache.
You see, a toothache hurts and the only way
to fix it is to do something about it. We all know it,
but we put it off because we're afraid it'll hurt worse.
But once that tooth is gone, you'll feel a whole lot better."

—*Pastor Frank Hogan*

*A*bigail Stanton was no stranger to heartbreak. When her husband and son died in the mining accident, her world was torn apart. She had every right to be mad—mad at the world and at the Pacific Northwest Mining Company for putting the men to work in unsafe conditions. Later, when a wood plank was found in the collapsed mine with the words "Forgive me, Pa" on it, Abigail immediately recognized her husband's handwriting. That word "forgive"—to let go of a grievance—is a loaded concept.

Noah Stanton's last words to his wife were "Forgive me." Abigail had been able to do that a year ago. Which meant she was ready to open her heart again. This time to Mountie Bill Avery, the forensic investigator sent to find out how the mining disaster had happened. And he had proved the mining company was at fault for the deaths of the men. In doing so, he became a hero to the town … and also won Abigail's heart.

However, as is always the case, life is messy and heroes are flawed too. Bill hadn't been completely honest with Abigail. When she discovered a photograph of him with his wife and child, she confronted him, and he explained that he had lost them both.

But something wasn't adding up, and when a woman showed up at the cafe and introduced herself as Nora Avery, Bill's estranged wife, Abigail felt like she had been kicked by a horse. Now she had a whole new bucket of grievances she couldn't forgive. Every time she saw Bill in town, she turned and walked away. Bill tried to explain himself, but Abigail refused to listen. That's when Pastor Frank Hogan stepped in, recognizing Abigail's broken places, her anger, and unforgiving spirit. He encouraged her to let it go—not for Bill's sake, but her own.

Forgiving those who wrong us is hard to do. In Scripture, God tells us He forgives us, so we should do likewise with others. But sometimes it's easier to forgive complete strangers than it is to pardon people we care about who've hurt us. It's so easy to harbor anger and hold grudges, sometimes for years. But the truth is, grievances hurt us more than those we hold them against. Anger eats us up from the inside, and studies prove that bitterness robs us of good health, and even takes years off our lives.

Pastor Frank compared it to a decaying tooth. Until we completely yank it out, the hurt will never go away. So, as Abigail eventually did for Bill, the best way to live is to forgive often and much. And it will keep us out of the heavenly dentist chair too.

Prayer from the Heart

God, it's so hard to let anger go when people hurt us. It's so much easier to be angry and bitter. But I know that's not the life you want me to live. Please help me to realize that hurt people ... *hurt* people. Please help me to let go of my resentment and hatred. Let me forgive those who wrong me, just as you forgive me when I wrong you, Lord. Help me to show grace and mercy to those who have caused me pain in the past. Heal my broken places. Make me aware when I've hurt others. Thank you, God, for forgiving me of all my sins. May I work to live a grace-filled life that is pleasing to you.

⚜

What's on Your Heart Today?

- What hurt do you need to release today?

- How can letting go allow you to live a richer, fuller life?

- Some people are easy to forgive and others are more challenging. Why do you think you feel that way?

19

WELCOME TO THE HUMAN RACE

Yet to all who did receive him, to those
who believed in his name, he gave the right
to become children of God.

JOHN 1:12

"Tom, I believe in you."

—Jack Thornton

*T*om Thornton had a checkered past, and trouble always seemed to find him. His good looks and charisma made him attractive to the ladies—one lady in particular—Elizabeth's sister, Julie Thatcher, the youngest of the Thatcher girls. Her fiery red hair matched her personality. She was always looking for thrills and adventure. Tom was all that and more.

He wasn't a bad boy. Not really. He just lacked a strong male figure in his life to give him guidance ... and perhaps the gene for good judgment. Jack Thornton loved Tom, and was a great big brother, but as a Mountie, he was often far from home. Jack and Tom's father, who had also been a Mountie, died when the boys were young, and a rebellious, prodigal spirit seemed to be cast in Tom when his father died.

As much as Jack was on the straight and narrow in his duty as a Mountie, Tom seemed to be on a crooked path. Bar brawls and drunken late nights in a back-alley were not uncommon to the younger Thornton brother. Elizabeth's parents, the Thatchers—an upstanding family in Hamilton high society—did not see Tom as much of a match for their youngest daughter. Which meant that Tom and Julie were destined to be moths to the flame, because despite their opposite backgrounds, they had two flaws in common: self-absorption and impulsiveness. It's not too hard to predict a train wreck, or in this case, a car wreck just waiting to happen.

Tom wrestled with the kind of man he was supposed to be as he sat talking to Jack. He felt like his entire life had been a disappointment to his brother and their mother. But Jack reminded him how their father bragged about how much he loved Tom, and how he always considered Tom to be a chip off the old block. It was an opinion he really needed to hear, because fathers help tell us just who we are in this world. Or don't tell us, which leaves us searching for our identity.

Have you ever been so frustrated with the choices you've made in life that you didn't like looking in the mirror? Well, welcome to the human race. Maybe, like Tom and Julie, you haven't heard your father's official opinion about you. Or your heavenly Father's. But here it is: you are a child of the King, which makes you a prince or a princess. You are His beautiful creation—a unique masterpiece made in His image.

He loves you. Don't ever forget that. What you choose to do with that knowledge is up to you. Will you choose to make a difference?

Prayer from the Heart

Father, there are days when I look in the mirror and feel nothing but shame and disgust. I'm frustrated with the choices I've made or the words I've said to you and others. I know you've already forgiven me, but it's important I ask your pardon anyway. Please prompt me when I need to also ask the forgiveness of those who are affected by my choices. Help me to remember that I am your child. A child of the King of kings. Direct me to be the best me I can be. God, I want you to be proud of me for who I am, but I realize that you are proud of me because of *Whose* I am. I am yours.

⟳⟲

What's on Your Heart Today?

- When have you struggled with your identity?

- How does knowing you are a child of God help you see your own value?

- If you could do anything for God, what would it be?

20

JUST ASK

Because of the LORD's great love we are not consumed,
for his compassions never fail.
They are new every morning;
great is your faithfulness.

LAMENTATIONS 3:22–23

**"It really feels like we've been
given a second chance today."**
—*Elizabeth Thatcher*

*T*hings had been tense between Elizabeth Thatcher and Jack Thornton since returning from Hamilton (where they'd gone to visit Elizabeth's sick mother). Their backgrounds and families were just so different. When Elizabeth's father offered Jack a job with his company, Elizabeth was thrilled, but Jack was insulted. Why would he ever want a desk job when his life mission was to be a Mountie? Jack assumed Mr. Thatcher thought his role with the Royal Canadian Mounted Police wasn't respectable.

Jack and Elizabeth had been through rough spells before, but this time it seemed different. Even after their return to Hope Valley, their relationship remained strained. One day, when Elizabeth tried to talk to Jack about their conflict, he seemed preoccupied. Rip, his dog, had gone missing. That's when it hit Elizabeth. She had come looking for Jack earlier, and she might have inadvertently left the jailhouse door open.

Jack recalled where Rip had run the last time thunder spooked him: the old mine. With a storm now hitting as he and Elizabeth reached the mine, they decided to make a fire inside to wait out the weather. That's when they heard Rip howling in the distance. They split up, each taking a different shaft in search of the dog—only danger was looming. While Jack tracked down Rip in one tunnel, in Elizabeth's shaft, a wooden support beam gave way and knocked her to the ground. Her scream brought Jack running, and as he went to her aid, another beam fell. He quickly shielded her from the falling debris and they both rolled to safety.

In the aftermath, each of them were breathless from what

might have been. Elizabeth could have been hurt or even killed by that cave-in. Suddenly all their differences seemed petty in light of their love for each other. They had been given a second chance. At life. At love. A second chance to say exactly how they felt about each other.

Did you know that God is in the business of second chances? It's what He loves to do best. It doesn't matter how many first chances we've blown, He forgives us and removes our mistakes from us. Do you know far He removes them? The Bible says "as far as the east is from the west" (Psalm 103:12). That means God forgets our mistakes, and never again dredges them up. God breathes new life into rocky marriages, restores financial ruin, helps us overcome the consequences of wrong choices—or any of a thousand kinds of transgressions. All we have to do is ask.

No matter what you've done or what has happened in your life, God will never give up on you. His mercies are new every day.

Prayer from the Heart

God, I come before you humbled because I make so many mistakes. Each day I hope for a better start, yet I mess up again. Forgive me for the times I make choices that are not pleasing to you. Show me the areas of my life where there are offenses I don't even realize. You are a God of new beginnings. Thank you for the many times you have granted me a do-over. As many times as you've pardoned me and let me start over, grant me the grace to offer that same spirit of forgiveness and mercy to someone who has wronged me. Thank you for second chances, Lord. May I not take them for granted.

What's on Your Heart Today?

- Can you name a time in your life when God granted you a second chance?

- What did you do with the new chance you were given?

- How do God's second chances affect your ability to grant those same fresh starts to others?

❧ *21* ❧

"AULD LANG SYNE"

"Before I formed you in the womb I knew you,
before you were born I set you apart;
I appointed you as a prophet to the nations."

JEREMIAH 1:5

**"And with that another year passes and a new
year begins. A year for family. A year for truth.
A year for unexpected blessings and a year for love."**

—*Elizabeth Thatcher*

*R*osemary Leveaux wanted everything to be perfect for New Year's. Rosemary always wanted everything to be perfect, so she entered an essay contest with a big-city newspaper about her "frontier family and how they celebrate New Year's Eve." And guess what? She won. The prize? The newspaper would dispatch a reporter to profile Hope Valley about its New Year's celebration. Rosemary, who always basked in attention, could not have been more excited.

There were only two problems. Rosemary was a single lady with a boyfriend, Lee Coulter, but no family as of yet, and there was no New Year's celebration planned. She had spun the truth, so she needed to quickly create appearances to match her colorful essay.

So Rosemary dove right into the planning of the biggest event the town had ever seen. For starters, she wanted fireworks, a marching band, a children's play, and a time capsule. Rosemary bustled about town, encouraging everyone to get involved, running from planning committee to planning committee. She was a sight to behold.

When the reporter arrived early and unannounced, Rosemary was caught off guard because the reporter was anxious to meet her husband and hear about frontier life in a frontier town from a true frontier family. With her talent for talking people into doing her bidding, she coaxed Lee into posing as "Mr. Leveaux," her husband. He was not happy about fudging the truth and let her know it.

When Rosemary finally came clean to the reporter, he admitted he already knew. She confessed that while she didn't have a husband, she did have a family: the whole town of Hope Valley. The reporter decided he would still write his story because it was a town whose people cared about each other all year round.

Rosemary had wanted her life and circumstances to appear more glamorous and exciting than reality. Sometimes we do the same, right? We try to be something we aren't. We bustle around and run ourselves ragged trying to keep up with the Joneses because they seem to have everything we want. And in the process, our "Auld Lang Syne" becomes Auld Lang-xiety.

But with God, none of that is necessary. Did you know that the Scriptures tell us we are made in God's image and that we are His workmanship, created to do good things in this world? God knows our strengths and weaknesses. He smiles at our victories and stands ready to catch us when we fall. In other words, we don't have to create an essay-winning life to be accepted. He loves us just the way we are.

Prayer from the Heart

Father, sometimes I get caught up in appearances. When I see the lives of others, I want to compare myself with them. I want to look a certain way, dress a certain way, and act a certain way. But after a while, it's hard to keep on the mask. God, please help me to be more transparent. Let me always remember that you want me to come just as I am. You love me no matter what. Help me to live my life without masks. Help my life to not be about the show, but about you. Let me care more about pleasing you than pleasing other people. Heal my broken places and make me new. Thank you, Lord, for loving me unconditionally.

༄༅༅༄

What's on Your Heart Today?

- In what areas of your life do you struggle with comparisons?

- Think of someone you know who lives with transparency. How does their transparency make you respect them?

- How can you living with transparency help others in their journey?

22

Not *If* ... But *When*

"When you pass through the waters, I will be with you;
and when you pass through the rivers,
they will not sweep over you.
When you walk through the fire, you will not be burned;
the flames will not set you ablaze."

ISAIAH 43:2

"It feels like someone took something from you,
like there is a giant hole inside of you.
But one day that feeling that you're feeling right
now, that feeling is going to go away. I promise."

—*Jack Thornton*

*C*ody Hastings' start in Hope Valley wasn't an easy one. He and his older sister, Becky, had been making it on their own in the woods since their parents' death. But when Becky got sick, Cody took it upon himself to care for her. He would sneak into town, going from house to house, "borrowing" food and firewood. His best "supplier" of bakery goods was the cooling window at Abigail's Café—until the day Abigail caught him red-handed with one of her pies. But instead of turning Cody in as a runaway, she fed him, took him in, and insisted on helping Becky as well. Abigail recognized their need and met it.

After a visit, the doctor was concerned enough about Becky's health to recommend she return with him to the city hospital where she could get the proper medicine, which meant Cody would be all alone in a new town. Cody's new life living with Abigail and going to school with Miss Elizabeth Thatcher as his teacher got off to an inauspicious start.

Cody and Becky had lived on their own long enough that he had forgotten what it was like to follow rules. He was tardy to school and skipped his homework assignments. Abigail tried to be understanding, but when Cody got to roughhousing with his baseball inside Elizabeth's house and broke a vase Jack Thornton had given her as a housewarming gift, things got tense and Cody stormed out, unapologetic and angry.

Abigail, Jack, and Elizabeth all realized that the boy's emotions from losing his parents and feeling abandoned in a new town had overwhelmed him. He had pain, grief, and loss that was being expressed through anger and outbursts.

Cody felt the way many of us do sometimes. The phrase "It's not fair!" rolls easily off our tongues when life gets challenging, doesn't it? It's easy to believe and follow the rules when no adversity comes our way. But unfortunately, bad things happen to good people, and unlike in comic books, good guys don't always win.

That's life for all of us. God doesn't promise perpetual happy endings. But He does promise "When you pass through the waters, they will not sweep over you" (Isaiah 43:2). Notice it doesn't say *if* we pass through the waters, but *when* we do. So when storm clouds are threatening, and we feel like running away like Cody, remember that God will recognize our needs and meet them. He allows the storms. Without them, we would never have the blessing of His provision. And remember, He's also the God of blue skies, sunrises, and rainbows ... especially rainbows.

Prayer from the Heart

Father, there are times when I want to scream over the circumstances I'm facing. When the job I need or the money I've prayed for doesn't come in, or the people that I'm close to suffer or even pass away, it just doesn't seem fair. Please help me to remember that you never promised fair, but you did promise never to leave me or forsake me. Thank you, God, for always being near to me when I'm lonely or in pain. I know I am never truly alone. Help me to see your hand in every situation. Help me not to borrow tomorrow's trouble today by allowing worry to take over my life. Take my struggles and use them for your glory.

⚬⁄⚬⚬⚬

What's on Your Heart Today?

- In what situation have you felt frustrated because your circumstances didn't seem fair?

- How would life change if everything truly was fair? Would you rather have fairness or justice?

- How does knowing God is with you during the storms help you to get through them?

23

WANTED

Confess your trespasses to one another,
and pray for one another, that you may be healed.

JAMES 5:16A NKJV

"All the times you preached mercy and forgiveness,
they heard you. Maybe you just need to convince
them that everybody deserves a second chance.
Fight them. I'll stand with you."

—*Abigail Stanton*

When Pastor Frank Hogan came into town, he was everything Hope Valley could dream of in a spiritual leader. He was filled with grace and wisdom, kind to all who knew him, and always available to listen. People were drawn to his friendly face and unassuming ways.

No one suspected that Pastor Frank had a secret. After he and Abigail Stanton became friends, he responded with vague answers when she asked him about his past. He told her he almost died, and that motivated him to dedicate his life to God.

But soon, Pastor Frank's past came to find him. A young man named Jesse came to town looking for Matt Landry. Jesse soon found him. The ugly truth was that Pastor Frank was Matt Landry, at one time the powder man (explosives expert) for the Garrison gang. He and Jesse had worked together to commit robberies. The gang wanted their old colleague back to do a job for them and sent Jesse to convince him to rejoin them.

Frank Hogan's near-death experience was, in fact, true. The part he didn't mention was that he almost died as Matt Landry because he was shot and captured in a robbery. He served time in prison and was released. While behind bars, Matt found the Word of God, and it changed him. Upon his release, he legally changed his name as a sign that his old life was dead to him. As Frank Hogan, he was a new man. Hope Valley was his first congregation. Worried the town wouldn't accept his past, Frank kept quiet until Jesse flushed him out by nailing an old "Wanted" poster with Frank's picture on the door of Abigail's Café.

Mountie Jack Thornton did some checking and discovered that everything Frank had admitted was true. There were no active warrants out for either Matt Landry or Frank Hogan, and as far as he could tell, there was no law against changing your name. But the townspeople still spoke in whispers whenever he walked by. Finally, Abigail insisted that he come clean with the entire town. Let them hear the truth directly from him. After hearing his story of life transformation, the town voted unanimously for Frank to remain their pastor.

Are you haunted by mistakes in your past? Has shame forced you to become somebody you are not? Perhaps others have been unforgiving and that has made it hard for you to forgive yourself. If any of these describe your struggle, Scripture tells us that confession is good for the soul because speaking out about our wrongs gives us power over them. Remember, our past does not define us. We aren't our past mistakes. Yes, we are "Wanted" … *wanted* by a loving and Almighty God.

Prayer from the Heart

Lord, forgive me for the mistakes I've made in the past. I often focus on those blunders and then feel immobilized because I don't like what I see. Help me to remember that once I've been forgiven, you don't look at those faults anymore. Help me to forgive myself, and guide my eyes to focus on you. When I concentrate on you, I don't see my flaws. Instead, I see your grace which forgave me once and for all. Thank you, God, that my past does not define me. You've provided me a fresh start. Your Word even says you've given each of your children a new name. Thank you for forgiving me and making me new.

What's on Your Heart Today?

- What things in your past do you have a hard time letting go?

- Why do you spend so much time focusing on your flaws?

- How do you think God could use those past mistakes in a positive way?

24

BE SOMEONE'S HERO

For the LORD your God is the one who goes with you,
to fight for you against your enemies, to save you.

DEUTERONOMY 20:4 NASB

"I needed an ending to my story and I found one.
I found it in how the people of Hope Valley stood
together to face their problems and their fears."

—*Elizabeth Thatcher*

The Garrison gang wasn't about to take no for an answer from Pastor Frank Hogan. He had been their explosives man at a very different time in his life, and they needed him back for a heist they wanted to pull—a gold train ripe for the plundering.

They figured they could tarnish his name in Hope Valley by leaking his shady past and leading the citizens to run him out of town. And the closer the train got, the more desperate they were with their strong-arm measures. Nothing like greed to fuel determination. Late one night, a rock crashed through the window of Abigail Stanton's café. On it were the painted words "Matt Landry," Pastor Frank's "before God" name. The message was clear. The gang would not stop harassing the town until Matt Landry rejoined their group.

The town called a meeting to discuss the threat. Mayor Henry Gowen suggested they send out a posse to hunt down the gang, but Mountie Jack Thornton shot down the idea. He knew it would only result in innocent people getting hurt. The town finally agreed to have the men take turns keeping watch over the town around the clock.

The gang also kept watch. They had smuggled one of their own into the town to be their eyes and ears. Jesse Flynn seemed like a nice, unassuming young man, and he told Clara Stanton, the girl who had his eye, that the gang would kill Pastor Frank if he refused them any longer. But Clara saw something good in Jesse and convinced him to turn from his outlaw ways and help Jack apprehend the bandits.

Hope Valley needed a hero. In fact, many heroes. And

it took nearly every man in town to stand up and be counted as brave. In the end, the townspeople saved themselves and Pastor Frank. By banding together, they were able to capture the Garrison gang and stand behind their pastor—a man who once had been lost, but was now transformed by God.

Have you ever been someone's hero? At some point in our lives, God calls each of us to overcome our fears and stand up for what's right and just in our communities. That means speaking out against what may be popular, convenient, or expedient, or what goes against God's laws. It means we can't always get along or go along with things just because it's easier.

The Bible says to stand firm in our faith, to be courageous and strong. It's always scary to step up like that, but here's the good news: God will go with us into that battle. He will fight for us, and with us, and never leave our side.

Prayer from the Heart

God, I'm in need of courage. There are days when I feel I'm drowning in details or on a merry-go-round that won't slow down. I sure don't feel like a hero, but I know you've called me to step up and be one for you—because we live in a world that's in desperate need of truth-tellers and torchbearers. Can I do that? Not with how much I doubt myself. But my strength comes from knowing that you will go with me, that you'll speak for me, and that you'll hold my hand through it all. Thank you for being my ultimate Hero and for hearing me when I call to you. Let me be brave, in your name.

What's on Your Heart Today?

- Where do you need rescue right now?

- Why do you think people generally have a hard time asking for help?

- Has God ever called you to be a hero? In what ways has God used you to help rescue other people?

25

LOVING THE UNLOVELY

And be kind to one another, tenderhearted, forgiving
one another, even as God in Christ forgave you.

EPHESIANS 4:32 NKJV

"It doesn't matter who started it.
What's important is that we all learn
to treat each other with kindness."

—*Elizabeth Thatcher*

Simply put, Hattie Ferguson was an obnoxious kid. Elizabeth Thatcher had just introduced her as a new student, and her less-than-pleasant response hadn't endeared her to anyone. None of the children seemed to be getting along, so Elizabeth announced, "Today will be the first day of Kindness Week. Every day this week your homework is to do something kind for someone."

Later, when the townswomen were chatting about the upbringing of Hope Valley's kids, Rosemary Leveaux mentioned her belief that the best way to teach children manners was to hold a dance. Within minutes, decorations, refreshments, and plans for a dance class had all come together.

Then Rosemary sprung it on the children, and announced that after-school dance lessons would begin immediately. When Hattie didn't respond well to the news of the dance, Opal Weise tried to comfort her by offering to let her hold her beloved stuffed bear, Brownie—but Hattie threw the cuddle toy to the ground. Elizabeth reprimanded her and suggested that spurning kindness from a classmate was not the way to make friends. Elizabeth then told her a story about when she first arrived in Hope Valley, "I didn't have any friends. But then I learned that the people here are kind, generous, and caring. You just need to give them a chance."

But Hattie was still struggling. When Rosemary began the dance lessons, Cody Hastings asked Hattie if he could have the first dance, and once again she responded rudely.

At wit's end, Elizabeth decided she needed to talk with Hattie's mother. At school, Hattie had put on airs, inferring that she was from a wealthy family, and often mentioning she didn't need any friends besides her best friend, Janie, from back home. But Hattie's mother revealed a different story—they were not only struggling to make ends meet, but Janie had passed away recently. Elizabeth realized Hattie was pretending in order to cover up how much she was hurting.

Do you have an antagonistic person in your life? It's hard to love the unlovely, and we often find ourselves avoiding them. But sometimes that's the worst way to respond. When our feelings get hurt, it's easy to lash back with our own hurtful words. But the Bible says that a soft answer turns away anger. There is always a deeper reason for an obnoxious person's behavior. Maybe they've been scarred by childhood experiences, or they're lonely, or they've never experienced authentic friendship or love. Which likely means God has placed us in their lives for a reason—so we can demonstrate His love to them. That makes us His hands and feet in that relationship. Kindness, generosity, and tender loving care heals a hurting heart every time.

Prayer from the Heart

Lord, sometimes I forget that there are hurting people all around me. Open my eyes to someone you want me to love. Remind me that anger is more than skin deep. Help me to look below the surface for the pain of a wounded soul instead of just focusing on a grouchy exterior. You have always given me grace that I don't deserve, so help me offer that in return to those who are hurting, even if they show me no grace. Give me a tender and loving heart. Help me to keep responding with kindness no matter what. Father, I'm grateful for your love and patience with me. Help me to love like you do, and help others to see you in me.

What's on Your Heart Today?

- Why are people sometimes hateful and grouchy?

- Why is it sometimes so hard to be kind to those people?

- What are some specific ways you can dispense kindness to them?

26

YOUR ONE THING

"But as for you, be strong and do not give up,
for your work will be rewarded."

2 CHRONICLES 15:7

"Sometimes our smallest actions
lead to our biggest victories."
—*Elizabeth Thatcher*

Rosemary Leveaux had taken Hope Valley by storm. The moment she'd stepped off the stagecoach two years before, her dramatic flair became apparent to all who met her. Years earlier, she'd been betrothed to Jack Thornton before breaking the engagement to pursue her acting career. A natural-born actress, Rosemary thrived in any spotlight people were willing to shine on her.

Not long after her arrival, Rosemary had the chance to show off her skills by directing the children in the Founder's Day play. As soon as Lee Coulter opened his sawmill in Hope Valley, Rosemary begged him to build a theater so she could stretch her wings. Which meant that when Rosemary heard the Omnigraph Moving Picture Company was coming to Hope Valley to shoot a motion picture, she assumed she'd be a shoo-in for a plum role.

She couldn't wait to reveal her talents to the director. When she spotted him scouting the town, Rosemary made a grand introduction, proclaiming, "I am an actress." The director, Mr. Pope, quickly informed her that all the roles were already filled. Rosemary was befuddled. How could he turn her down? She was stunned when she discovered that Lee Coulter's assistant, Mike Hickam, Mary Dunbar, and Molly Sullivan had already won parts.

Feeling like the ship had sailed without her, Rosemary found a spot to sulk. When Lee saw her, he encouraged her to show the director the magnitude of her passion for acting. And so she found Mr. Pope and offered to perform a soliloquy from any play he could name. He tried to dismiss her until

Rosemary made it personal. "Have you ever wanted something so much that you thought your heart would simply stop beating if you didn't get it?" It was that heartfelt appeal that caused Mr. Pope to give Rosemary a tiny role.

What one skill or talent has God given you that you are more passionate about than anything else in your life? What dream gets you up in the morning or keeps you awake at night? God made you in His image. That means you have a tiny strand of the DNA of the Creator of the universe, and He wants you to strive to be the Michelangelo of that one thing. Scripture tells us when we commit our work to God, He will establish our plans.

If there is something that we know God has called us to do, there is no such thing as God suddenly "uncalling" us. Remember that He didn't ask us to be successful—He asked us to be faithful. Let's not give up ... because when God gives us a dream, a "no" from this world will still mean a "yes" from Him.

Prayer from the Heart

Father, thank you for the gift you have given me. Sometimes I feel like my heart will burst if I don't get to use it. Give me the determination to continue growing and learning what I need to achieve my dreams. May my dreams align with your will for my life. Help me not to focus on myself, but instead, to keep my eyes on you. Help me to remember that all gifts come from you and that I need to use them for your purposes, not my own. And if it be your will, connect me with the right people and send me divine appointments. Lord, give me the courage to move forward for you.

What's on Your Heart Today?

- What gifts has God given you?

- How can you use those gifts to bring God glory?

- If you could do anything with the talents you've been given, what would you do?

27

THE BETTER YES

The heart of man plans his way,
but the LORD establishes his steps.
PROVERBS 16:9 ESV

"I guess it's time to say goodbye."
—*Abigail Stanton*

*B*ecky and Cody Hastings had just settled into living with Abigail Stanton when Caroline Connors—the children's aunt—showed up in Hope Valley without any warning. She'd hired an investigator to find her niece and nephew after she learned of her sister's death. Even though they'd never met her, she planned to take the kids to live with her in Davenport.

Abigail was upset that Caroline gave Becky and Cody the news without her. Despite the fact that they were also distraught, Caroline gave Abigail until Tuesday to have them packed to leave. The decision devastated Abigail. How could she let go of these precious children she loved so much?

At breakfast, Caroline tried to persuade the kids that coming to live with her would be in their best interests. She told Cody about the wonderful house they would live in, and shared how Becky would be a debutante and would no longer have to worry about studying science and math. But she did not realize that this news only troubled the kids. As the day neared for their departure, Caroline was confused by their unhappiness. She was stunned when Becky won the science fair and the judge advised that she should think about attending a technical university to help develop her talents.

As everyone gathered at the stagecoach to say goodbye, the scene was beyond poignant. Tears filled many eyes as Opal Weise offered Cody her beloved bear, Brownie, as protection for his travels, and Abigail thought her heart would break as she clung to Cody for one last hug.

But then, in a stunning act of love, Caroline had a change of heart. She said she wanted what was best for the children, telling Cody he could stay with Abigail, and promising Becky that she would make sure she could go to the technical school of her dreams.

Letting go is never easy, and often painful. But when God asks us to turn loose of something we hold precious, with either a convicting message from Scripture, or a deep prompting on our hearts, we should listen. That's because the Author of all things writes the stories of our lives. He knows the twists and turns that lie ahead. It's only when our hands are empty and in an open position that God can fill them with the new thing that He has planned for us.

When God writes a new chapter for our lives, it's not because He wants to take something away or wants to say "no." It's because He wants us to say the "better yes" to what He has waiting for us.

Prayer from the Heart

Father, when you ask me to let go of something, forgive me for so often digging my heels in and hanging on for dear life. It's hard to let go of what I love. Sometimes it's not just rebellion that keeps me from doing that, it's that I have a hard time trusting that you have my best interests in mind. Help me to embrace that whenever you ask me to give something up, it's usually because you have something more precious waiting for me. Please help me to be willing and help me to be obedient to whatever you ask of me. Thank you for being a faithful God and for being with me in every situation.

What's on Your Heart Today?

- How can letting go sometimes be a sacrifice you make for others?

- How can trust be a big issue when it comes to letting go?

- How can letting go sometimes be a blessing in disguise?

28

HEAVENLY SALVE

"Do to others as you
would like them to do to you."
Luke 6:31 NLT

"When two people feel that way about each other,
they find answers. And finding the answers brings
them together. It doesn't pull them apart."
—*Elizabeth Thatcher*

She arrived in the rain after dark and knocked on the jail-house door. Jack Thornton didn't expect to see who was under the rim of the dripping wet cowboy hat. It was none other than his mother—Charlotte Thornton. She had obviously ridden a great distance through a storm to visit her son. She wanted to find out more about the schoolteacher, Elizabeth Thatcher, who he'd spoken of in his letters home.

Jack could only shudder nervously at the thought of these two lady comets he loved colliding the next morning. And when they did, their differences were polar opposite. Charlotte was a woman's woman who could ride, shoot, and hunt. She even made her own clothes—including her leather riding chaps. As rough and tough as she was, Elizabeth was polished, refined, and genteel. Wanting to both impress and get to know the older woman, Elizabeth invited Charlotte to stay in her home for the duration of her visit.

Elizabeth volunteered to cook dinner for the trio that evening. But before she could finish making the Shepherd's Pie, Charlotte added a healthy spoonful of lard, claiming that lard is the universal secret to all cooking. Even though she wasn't much of a cook herself, Elizabeth knew that this was a mistake, but bit her tongue. At dinner, Jack went through torture trying to choke down the meal with a grateful grin on his face.

The next morning, Charlotte also found it disappointing that Elizabeth wasn't an early riser, and that she didn't do her own laundry. From Elizabeth's perspective, it seemed Charlotte was determined to belittle her every chance she got. From Charlotte's vantage point, it seemed that Elizabeth was a pampered princess. But through all of Charlotte's criticisms, Elizabeth did something very few of us could do: She smiled and responded with kindness. Their differences were clear, but Elizabeth recognized the importance of trying to maintain a good relationship with Jack's mother.

Who in your life gets on your nerves? How do you respond when that happens? Most of the time, we can just simply walk away and choose not to be around people who grate on us. But when a source of irritation is actually a close family member, sometimes we don't have a choice but to paste on a smile and swallow our frustration.

God's way of dealing with His children in all their moods is to show them love. For us, sometimes that means sacrificing our own needs in order to love the unlovable. And even when they are incapable of reciprocating—God will reciprocate by applying His heavenly salve to take away the sting of hurtful behavior and to bind the wounds on our souls.

Prayer from the Heart

God, there are people who just rub me the wrong way sometimes. Criticism is always on their lips. Even when they give a compliment, it sometimes feels like an insult. Father, help me to get along with these people. And show me when I am being an irritant to someone else. Let me know when to keep my mouth shut, and when to speak truth. Help me to treat others the way I would like to be treated, and not necessarily the way they treat me. When people are rude, help me to always respond with love. Thank you for loving me and showing me how you want me to respond to others. Let me show grace in the same way that you do.

⟨ۇﻮﭴﯙ⟩

What's on Your Heart Today?

- Who is that "sandpaper" person in your life who rubs you the wrong way?

- Think of some things they have said to you in the past. What are some grace-filled responses you could use for the future?

- Why do you think critical people are so quick to point out the flaws in others?

29

THE BEST PLACE TO BE

"Then you will call upon Me and go and pray to Me,
and I will listen to you."

JEREMIAH 29:12 NKJV

"The whole town is praying for you."
—*Elizabeth Thatcher*

*T*he news from the Silverton Mine wasn't good. A landslide had taken out the mine, shades of another tragedy a few years ago at the Coal Valley mine. Jack Thornton gathered men to ride out there with him. When they arrived, things were grim. Men were trapped, dozens were injured, and two had died.

Back in town, the women gathered supplies and got cots ready at the schoolhouse where Nurse Faith set up a temporary infirmary. Abigail Stanton and Elizabeth Thatcher headed out to the settlement to comfort the families of the trapped miners. Everyone was frightened. But the danger wasn't over. The landslide caused a logjam on the river which now sent threatening floodwaters toward the settlement. Abigail and Elizabeth's mission now changed to helping settlers evacuate. Panic ensued when they couldn't find one of Elizabeth's students, Maggie Lawson. She'd gone to retrieve a stuffed toy bear that she'd forgotten at the river.

Jack volunteered to go search for the child, and when he got there, he was relieved to find her and get her to high ground. But then his horse spooked and he was thrown into the creek just as the roaring floodwaters hit, knocking him unconscious and carrying him downstream.

Elizabeth's blood ran cold when a settler rode into town with Maggie, who confirmed a wall of water had swept Jack away. Elizabeth raced to join a search team at the river, and when they finally located Jack, he was partially submerged in the receding floodwaters. They carried his inert body back to town where Faith diagnosed a severe case of pneumonia.

And while Elizabeth and Jack's mother sat vigil by his bedside, Pastor Frank held a candlelight service in the street outside. The entire town gathered to pray for Jack.

Moments later as Elizabeth wept over him and talked quietly to him, Jack opened his eyes and began making a slow recovery.

It's difficult to have faith when the landslides and floods of life hit. And sometimes it's easy to get so discouraged by our circumstances that we don't even have the will to pray. But that's exactly when we need to pray most. When life gets hard, the best place to be is on our knees. And if we do that, do you know what the Bible promises? That God will be right there with us, listening to every word we utter. It also says when faithful people pray in earnest, big things can happen. Even in the times when God seems silent or we don't understand His answers, we can always trust His heart. As Jack and Elizabeth would agree—prayer works wonders ... especially when our hearts are linked together lifting our needs to heaven.

Prayer from the Heart

Lord, it's scary when someone I love is in the hospital or when I receive bad news from the doctor. My heart breaks when I watch my loved ones make bad choices. And sometimes when circumstances arrive that I can't control or when my finances are in dire straits, it feels like I can barely breathe. Those are the times that test me, but they're also the situations that draw me closer to you. I'm grateful for the gift of prayer, for being able to come to you with whatever is on my heart, and for your promise that you are in control. Thank you for the peace that you give me during difficult times, and for never leaving my side.

❦

What's on Your Heart Today?

- Why is prayer such a priceless gift?

- How can prayer give us peace during difficult times?

- What are some instances where you've seen prayer make a difference?

c~ 30 ~c

THE PERFECT MEDICINE

Let each of you look out not only for his own interests,
but also for the interests of others.

PHILIPPIANS 2:4 NKJV

"I'm kind of glad the freight train didn't
come through. I always knew the people
of Hope Valley really cared about each other,
but I never realized how much."

—*Elizabeth Thatcher*

*C*hristmas had definitely arrived in Hope Valley, but it had been a difficult year for their neighbors as folks from the settlement saw their homes destroyed in a flood and lost loved ones. Elizabeth Thatcher summed up the community's response best, "In the true spirit of giving, our town has joined together, promising to those less fortunate a holiday filled with comfort and joy."

She ordered a long list of gifts and supplies at Yost's Mercantile, buying extra things for the residents in the settlement. Jack Thornton promised Elizabeth that he'd find all of them a permanent home by Christmas, and he intended to deliver.

The honeymooners, Lee and Rosemary Coulter, returned from New York and brought Cody Hastings a ball autographed by the best pitcher in professional baseball. He loved it. The school was a whirl of activity as the children made decorations and practiced for a nativity pageant. Elizabeth even ordered special costumes from Hamilton.

All their plans were in high gear until Mr. Yost brought a telegram. Due to a train derailment, no deliveries would be made before Christmas. What would Elizabeth tell the children?

She couldn't let them be disappointed, so she and Jack met with the townspeople and inspired them to build toys and make costumes. Everyone raided their pantries for supplies. They worked all night to get the task done. Cody didn't want Maggie to be sad, so he traded his beloved ball for the special doll she'd wanted.

That night, the town gathered as the greatest story ever told was shared by children in robes and homemade angel costumes. Residents from the settlement walked into their warm new homes. The kids all enjoyed their handmade toys. And none of it would have happened if love hadn't stepped in.

Sometimes we forget it doesn't always cost a lot to make a difference in someone's life. Money isn't always the answer. Sometimes, gifts of our time and talents can ease someone's pain, encourage their hearts, or brighten their days. God provides us the best example, because Christmas is when perfect love came into the world. God gave what was most precious to Him—His Son—and he did it willingly because *we* are precious to Him.

If you're feeling blue or sad, did you know that there is a fast-acting medicine that can fix you right up? It's called "doing something for someone else." It works by helping you take your eyes off your own problems. As the citizens of Hope Valley learned, great joy can be found in giving and doing for others. And guess what? When we practice that kind of generosity, somehow we always seem to get back way more than we give away.

Prayer from the Heart

Father, help me to be an encourager and to share your love with others. Give me eyes that can see those who need a helping hand or a kind word. Deepen the well of compassion in me. Help me to get past my own selfish heart that always thinks about my needs first, and give me a heart that overflows with generosity as I look for ways that I can help someone else. Thank you for the times I've been the beneficiary of kindness from others. Bless them for blessing me. Most of all, thank you for your limitless love that touches my life in so many ways, and for the comfort and security that it brings me.

What's on Your Heart Today?

- What are some specific things you could do to be a blessing to someone?

- How could you inspire other people to join with you for a good cause?

- How does God's love paint a beautiful picture of how we can love others?

31

GETTING PAST THE PAST

Do not remember the former things,
nor consider the things of old.

ISAIAH 43:18 NKJV

"Spring has always been my favorite time of year.
It brings the promise of happiness, new hope,
new life, new dreams, and nowhere is that
promise more real than it is in Hope Valley
on a beautiful spring morning."

—*Elizabeth Thatcher*

*T*he railroad in Hope Valley brought numerous new students to the school. Cyrus Rivera was one of them. The new children didn't seem to be meshing too well with the existing students, so Jack Thornton suggested a friendly competition—a baseball game. With Jack and Elizabeth Thatcher serving as coaches, they split up the class, blending new and old students onto teams.

Cyrus wasn't happy about it. He told Elizabeth that he loved baseball, but he couldn't play due to the brace on his knee which limited his ability to run. Cyrus's dad confirmed that although his son had hurt his knee in a tumble from a horse, he no longer needed the brace. For some reason, he was afraid to take it off.

Hoping to help him past his fears, Elizabeth asked Cyrus to be her assistant coach. She explained that he could help the other kids improve their baseball skills. Meanwhile, on Jack's team, he was stunned by how well Anna Hayford could pitch the ball. But that frustrated Cody—pitcher was his favorite position. However, Cyrus lifted Cody's spirits by telling him he was such a good player his team needed him at a more crucial position.

But when Cyrus offered to demonstrate to Anna how to throw a special pitch—his brace tripped him up and he fell. He was suddenly overwhelmed with embarrassment, but Elizabeth didn't let him stay there. She told him that he had a gift for helping the other kids believe in themselves—and it was time for him to do the same.

The big game soon arrived. When one of Elizabeth's

players went out with an injury, Elizabeth turned to Cyrus. He was the only one who could step in to bat. He took a deep breath and said okay. After two strikes, he smashed a homerun. As he ran around the bases, it was obvious he had finally conquered his fear.

Many of us are like Cyrus. We've gone through painful events, and we become so focused on our past troubles that we have a hard time moving on to the new dreams God has waiting for us. We allow fear to keep us stuck on the bench of old circumstances when God wants to get us up on our feet and running the race that He has planned for us.

Did you know that God has given you a specific purpose and calling to fulfill with your skills and talents? Have you let fear keep you from answering that call? If you've been leaning on the crutch of an old circumstance to keep you from pursuing your purpose, today's a great day to get back in the game.

Prayer from the Heart

Father, help me get my eyes off my past, quit wallowing in the things that once were, and start moving forward to my life that can be. Help me to forgive myself for my mistakes. Help me to stop holding grudges, resentments, and bitterness. I've let those things defeat me. But just as spring brings a fresh new beginning each year, help me to move ahead for the beautiful future you have planned for me. Help me to learn from my painful past, and then show me how I can use what I've learned to help others. Turn the moments that tested me into a testimony of what you can do in our lives. I want to finish well for you.

What's on Your Heart Today?

- Why do you think you have trouble getting beyond your past experiences?

- How can fear factor into this?

- What fresh new start does God have waiting for you?

32

BECOME A CHAMPION TO SOMEONE

"A new commandment I give to you,
that you love one another."

JOHN 13:34 NKJV

"To Elizabeth, with all my love, Jack."

Jack Thornton

Writing a book is hard work. Elizabeth Thatcher had already learned that lesson. What she was also learning was that waiting to hear back from publishers was even harder. After months of tedious labor, she'd finished her manuscript and had sent it off to six publishers. The days since then had seemed as slow as molasses on a cold winter day. She made frequent trips to Yost's Mercantile, but on each occasion, there was nothing waiting for Elizabeth in the mail slot.

Then, finally, a letter came. That night, as she and Jack Thornton were having dinner at her house, she handed him the unopened envelope—she hadn't had the nerve to open it. She was hoping Jack would read it for her. She watched and waited anxiously as he did. He hated to tell her, but it was a rejection letter. The news hit hard.

Jack paid his own visit to the mercantile, where Nurse Faith noticed that he was buying watercolor paints, art paper, and pencils. He was a bit cagey on the purpose of his purchase, which she found curious, and it was clear he was on some sort of secret mission.

Elizabeth would soon find out the nature of that mission when Jack presented her with a very special gift. He waited nervously to see her response when she realized what it was: a one-of-a-kind, hand-published book. The cover read, "*A Collection of Frontier Stories,* by Elizabeth Thatcher." The inscription inside read, "To Elizabeth, with all my love, Jack." But that wasn't all. He'd painstakingly painted illustrations to go with all her stories. There was love on every page, in every pencil mark or brush stroke. Her face said it all when he told her that her writing inspired him and he wanted to be her first publisher.

All of us need champions in our lives, individuals who will cheer us on when we're discouraged, who will help us discover our skills and talents, who will look us right in the eye and confirm a God-given gift or dream we should chase.

Are you discouraged today because you've been faithful to the task to which God has called you, and it feels like you're spinning your wheels? Or maybe something *is* happening—but it's not the response you wanted or expected.

Each of us needs a champion to speak wisdom into our journey. But likewise, we also need to become a champion, an extension of God's loving hands for someone else who needs encouragement. Just as Jack learned from his precious gift to Elizabeth, love paired with compassion and action can comfort a wounded heart, revive a defeated spirit, and inspire someone to keep going. For whom will you be a champion?

Prayer from the Heart

Father, your Word is a love letter to the world—to me. Thank you for the love on every page and for the abundance of your wisdom shared with the world. You know me, so you know that the desire of my heart is to please you, to fulfill the dreams you've given me. Honestly, it's hard when rejections come and I feel like I've failed. Remind me that you don't require success, but faithfulness and a willing heart. Help me to take what I learn from my difficult experiences so that I can be a champion for others who need someone to look them in the eye and affirm their gifts and dreams. And please send me a champion to do that for me.

⚜

What's on Your Heart Today?

- What specific steps could you take to show love to someone who's struggling?

- How can you inspire others by your actions?

- How does God's love paint a picture for you of what to do?

33

THE MOST DANGEROUS PRAYER

"But I have raised you up for this very purpose,
that I might show you my power and that my name
might be proclaimed in all the earth."

EXODUS 9:16

"The women of Hope Valley never shy away from a
challenge. Abigail Stanton might never have intended
to serve as mayor, but she rose to the occasion and
made a deal with the National Pacific Railroad to
bring us progress and prosperity."

—*Elizabeth Thatcher*

*A*bigail Stanton was facing some complex decisions. Her new role as interim mayor was challenging, and multiple hard choices had to be made. One of those included whether to reject the National Pacific Railroad's land proposal—which made some of the town happy, and others mad. Abigail talked to the railroad's representative in Hope Valley, Ray Wyatt, and suggested a compromise. She offered to sell him a different tract of land than the one he had his eye on—at half price. When he balked, she also informed him that her offer would expire the moment she walked out the door. With his back to a corner, Ray accepted the terms, but he clearly wasn't happy being strong-armed by a woman.

Abigail's anxiety only increased with a report from Elizabeth Thatcher that with all the new families that had moved to Hope Valley and all the new students in the school, there weren't enough books to go around. She needed more funds. Abigail wished she could make that happen, but every aspect of the town's budget was stretched to the breaking point.

At her café, things were a little chaotic for Abigail, as well. New hire, Rosemary Coulter, seemed to be more interested in sketching dresses for Dottie Ramsey's dress shop than washing dishes and cooking customers' meals. Abigail worked out her stress by aggressively chopping some innocent carrots.

But despite the challenges, Abigail thrived in all her roles because God had designed her for those exact moments. He'd given her strength and wisdom. And all her life experiences leading up to now had given her a deep well of leadership to draw on. She had been prepared for just such a time as this.

Sometimes we move toward our goals with great enthusiasm. We have a plan and the confidence to put them into action. But if we aren't careful, it's easy to forget something important: the mission is God's, not ours. And He puts us in positions of power, on purpose, for *His* purpose. He wants to use our skills and abilities to make the world a better place for the welfare of other people and to fight injustice. Sometimes fear, stress, anxiety, and self-doubt can paralyze, preventing us from accomplishing His purpose. That's why we need to keep focused—not on our own weaknesses and limitations—but on what He can do with us and through us ... even when all we bring to Him is just a willing heart. Think about that.

The most dangerous prayer you will ever pray is this: "God, use me." When you do that, look out, He's about to make you a world changer—warts, weaknesses, worries, and all.

Prayer from the Heart

Lord, it boggles my mind that the God of the universe has a plan for little old me. I don't want to let you down. Give me single-minded focus to stay on point for what you've called me to do. Equip me with what I need. Provide wisdom and strength. I don't want your plan to be left undone because I'm afraid of failure. Help me to listen to your voice instead of those who would try to discourage me. And help me to make a difference with my life in this world. Use me in whatever way you want, and give me the courage not to shrink back from any job you put in front of me, no matter how big or small.

✦✦✦

What's on Your Heart Today?

- What purposes has God designed just for you?

- Why do you worry about failing, and what should you focus on instead?

- What can you do to help others see God's power?

⊶ 34 ⊷

ADVERSITY DOESN'T DEFINE US

We are hard-pressed on every side, yet not crushed;
we are perplexed, but not in despair; persecuted,
but not forsaken; struck down, but not destroyed.
2 CORINTHIANS 4:8–9 NKJV

**"The budget is not the only thing
stretched to its breaking point."**
—Abigail Stanton

*A*dversity had swept through Hope Valley like an icy wind on a winter day, and it was left to Abigail Stanton to deal with it as interim mayor. A budget crisis, complaints from townspeople, and dealing with some not-so-nice executives from the railroad all took a toll. But that was nothing compared to her shock when the charges against Mayor Henry Gowen were dropped and he reclaimed his job as mayor—quickly undoing all the good she had accomplished. Even Abigail's relationship with Pastor Frank Hogan was under duress. It's strange how pain can be so contagious.

Meanwhile, with all the new students in her classroom, Elizabeth Thatcher was still struggling to make ends meet. Overcrowding and book and supply shortages were the new norm. Since most of the new kids came with the arrival of the railroad workers, she decided to let Ray Wyatt know she didn't think the railroad was pulling its weight. When he responded with scorn, she threatened to take it to the newspaper. Ray was convinced that Elizabeth had gotten too big for her petticoat and he planned to bring her back down to size.

Hardship had hit Carson Shepherd before his arrival in Hope Valley, breaking his heart, and leaving him a defeated man. But in that way in which so many of us respond, he'd just packed up his trouble and brought it with him.

Misfortune had also taken up residence at the Cantrell home when Phillip's mother died while giving birth to him. Phillip told Elizabeth his father blamed him for his mother's death, that it was the reason his father didn't love him. When

Elizabeth tried to talk to Shane Cantrell, he broke her heart by taking Phillip out of school.

And in a gut-wrenching moment of adversity, when Elizabeth returned to the schoolhouse to retrieve her forgotten shawl, she was startled to discover a strange man writing "Mr. Stoneman" on her very own chalkboard. When she asked what he was doing, he told her he was preparing his lesson for the next day. With the newly reinstalled Mayor Gowen's help, Ray had gotten his revenge by replacing her.

As they say in the West, "Trouble rides a fast horse."

How about in your life? How do you deal with those unexpected moments of unfairness and injustice? Do you let it define you, or do you chalk it up to hardening your resolve, faithfulness, and character? The Bible says we need to be joyful even when we encounter trials, because the testing of our faith produces endurance. Just like the folks in Hope Valley, quitting and failure in times of challenge are never an option. And when we take on that attitude, we can be an unstoppable force for good.

Prayer from the Heart

Father, I know to expect adversity. I realize that hardships can defeat me if I let them. Lord, even in those times when it feels like a runaway wagon has slammed into me, help me to bounce back with purpose and courage. There have been situations where I've questioned you, but help me to remember that you only allow me to go through tough times to make me stronger. Light a fire in my heart so that I'll keep serving you no matter what comes my way. When difficulties arrive, remind me that you haven't forsaken me. Help me to spring back from those times stronger, wiser, and even more committed to doing my best for you.

❧❦❧

What's on Your Heart Today?

- How do you respond when adversity arrives in your life?

- How can you get past the despair of those moments?

- How can you use the lessons learned from difficult times?

35

HONEY, NOT VINEGAR

See that no one repays anyone evil for evil,
but always seek to do good to one another
and to everyone.

1 THESSALONIANS 5:15 ESV

"I know in my heart, God intended me
to be a teacher, Jack. It's who I am in my soul.
It's *why* I am."

—*Elizabeth Thatcher*

When Elizabeth Thatcher confronted Mayor Henry Gowen about why he replaced her with Mr. Stoneman in the classroom, he produced a letter from Thomas Higgins, Superintendent of Schools. Higgins said that she had used her family's influence and money to secure her teaching assignment. But Elizabeth had a different version of events. Mr. Higgins had written the letter out of spite because she had spurned his romantic advances.

But now that the letter was public, Elizabeth knew that her reputation, and quite possibly her teaching career—which she loved as much as anything in this world—was in jeopardy. Not only that, but Mr. Stoneman was a stern taskmaster with her beloved students. He had no tolerance for mistakes, no grace for children learning at their own speed. And, certainly, not one ounce of humor. He expected the students to memorize their homework, gave out demerits, and confiscated Brownie the Bear from little Opal Weise, leaving her in tears. And he snapped Emily Montgomery's pencil because she wasn't holding it correctly.

Worst of all, he expelled young Phillip Cantrell, accusing the boy of being "slow" and not keeping up with the other kids. Elizabeth tried reasoning with Mr. Stoneman, telling him that each student has unique needs. But Stoneman was not to be convinced. He told Elizabeth that she had coddled the children and was unfit to teach. And he reminded her she was no longer their teacher.

In response, Cody Hastings announced that he was done with school, and several other children showed up at Abigail's

Café, begging Elizabeth to tutor them. Elizabeth had every reason to be angry at Mr. Stoneman too. Teaching was her life—it's what God had intended her to be—and it had been taken away from her. But instead of joining the kids' protest movement, she did the unexpected. She told the children that Mr. Stoneman was their teacher and that they needed to be respectful of him. She encouraged them to be on their best behavior for him.

When people say things about us that aren't true, when their actions bruise us, it's always easier to lash back in frustration. But Scripture counsels us that a gentle answer turns away anger. The trumped-up charges against Elizabeth could have made her bitter, but she chose the high road. She offered the olive branch instead of the saber, and ultimately her teaching position was restored.

What do you offer those who've hurt you? Do you return kindness for hostility, or just more hostility? Sometimes the best way to fix a broken relationship is to be the first one to be the peacemaker. It may not be the world's way, but it is God's way. As Abigail Stanton says, "You always catch more flies with honey than vinegar."

Prayer from the Heart

Lord, when I'm unjustly accused of something, why is my first response always anger? I know in my heart it's wrong, but it's hard not to be bitter. Please show me how to respond with grace and to have the heart of a peacemaker. Fix the situations I get in, according to your will. Help me to learn what you want to teach me from these experiences, and help me to forgive, even when it isn't merited. Thank you for forgiving me on so many occasions when I haven't deserved it. Help me to respond in a manner that will please you. I know that others are often watching my life. Let them see your grace in all that I do.

⚜

What's on Your Heart Today?

- When you're treated unjustly, how does responding with anger affect you?

- What can you teach others by how you respond?

- Why does God tell us to repay evil with good?

36

TAKE A WALK WITH ME

For you *are* a holy people to the LORD your God;
the LORD your God has chosen you to be
a people for Himself, a special treasure
above all the peoples on the face of the earth.

DEUTERONOMY 7:6 NKJV

**"The same God that's called you to teach
has called me to serve my country."**

—Jack Thornton

Jack Thornton and Elizabeth Thatcher were following their callings, so why did there have to be so many heart-aches along the way? As a Mountie, Jack had already struggled with staying behind in Hope Valley while the young officer he'd mentored, Corporal Douglas Burke, took the assignment that had previously been offered to him. Doug led a battalion of men into battle against a notorious army of gun-runners in the Northern Territory. When news arrived of his death, Jack was devastated.

On his way through Hope Valley, Superintendent Sam Collins told Jack things were growing worse up north, and asked him again to take the assignment he'd rejected earlier. Jack was deeply torn. When he finally decided to go, he prayed for strength. Even harder would be telling Elizabeth.

She could never have been prepared to hear Jack's news, and she was utterly crushed. He tried to help her understand that he was only following his call, but Elizabeth ran off in tears. Heartbroken, she went to the pond and prayed for her own strength to get through this horrible chapter in their rela-tionship. When she talked to Abigail Stanton about it, Abigail reminded her that Jack was chosen to fight the good fight. Elizabeth knew she was right, but knowing it and accepting it were two very different things.

On the evening before he had to leave, Jack asked Elizabeth to take a walk with him to her schoolhouse—now beautifully candlelit. He'd prepared it so he could propose to her. It was both the happiest and saddest moment of her life, because the next day, Jack rode off into the unknown.

God chose Elizabeth to teach, and God chose Jack to serve his country. So why did they face such heartbreak when they were both doing exactly what God had called them to do? Why do *we* face similar challenges when we try following our call in life? Heeding a call is always hard, but we need to remember that the Author of the universe wrote the chapters of our lives before the beginning of time.

He is the Alpha and the Omega. That means He sees all our days from His vantage point in timeless eternity, and He knew how our story would end before He even wrote it. He knows the plot twists and the lessons we need to learn. And though we rarely see it at the time, what sometimes seems like the worst possible circumstances are actually meant to bless us—not harm us.

It's in those moments that we discover just how faithful God really is. And the last time we checked, there's nothing in the Bible that includes the words "... and then God failed me."

Prayer from the Heart

Lord, I'm doing what I feel like you've called me to do, but sometimes I struggle with understanding why the journey is so difficult and why I often have to wait so long to fulfill the task you've chosen for me. Give me patience in the waiting. Instead of whining when hard circumstances come, help me to draw closer to you. Show me what you want me to learn during the times you make me wait. Teach me the lessons you have for me during the challenging moments. Thank you for trusting me and choosing me to do this for you. Help me to finish the journey well and to leave nothing undone that you had planned for me.

ᘓᕷᘔ

What's on Your Heart Today?

- How does it make you feel to know that God chose you to fulfill part of His plan?

- Why do you think He sometimes sends challenges your way or makes you wait?

- How can you use these experiences to help others?

37

BE THE MIRACLE

He heals the brokenhearted
and binds up their wounds.

PSALM 147:3 NASB

"Just remember when people are mean,
chances are it's because they're unhappy, so they try
to make other people just as unhappy as they are."

—*Abigail Stanton*

*T*wo new students walked in the schoolhouse door. Earl and Chad Wyatt were nephews of the railroad man, Ray Wyatt. Their dad also worked for the railroad, and apparently, their mother had passed away. It was quickly obvious to Elizabeth Thatcher that the boys needed a major attitude adjustment.

When Earl took Brownie, her beloved stuffed bear, from Opal Weise at recess and wouldn't give him back, Cody Hastings tried to rescue it, but a tug of war between the two boys resulted in Brownie getting torn. When Elizabeth tried to intervene, Earl mouthed off to her. She told him she'd be talking to his uncle, due to the fact that their father was always on the road.

Of course, Ray just brushed her off when she told him about the boys' bullying ways at school. Elizabeth was getting a picture of why they were acting out, but she was never the kind of teacher to give up on a student.

Later in town, she tried a new tack with the younger brother, Chad, by inviting him to play with Cody and his dog, Dasher. Elizabeth said that perhaps this could be a fresh start for Chad. She also suggested that he might like to share something important to him for Show and Tell at school.

The following day, Chad showed up at school with a musical recorder, a flute-like instrument that had been given to him by his mother for Christmas. He said that although his mother had promised to teach him how to play, she never had. Elizabeth was stunned when it dawned on her that their mother hadn't died, she had actually abandoned Chad, Earl, and their father. She realized now why the boys acted like they did.

The experiences in our pasts affect all of us—in good ways and in bad. Sometimes when we peel back the layers of life, we discover that people who are particularly obnoxious or hostile toward us actually harbor deeply wounded hearts. Their unaddressed pain takes root and grows into bitterness, fear, and self-doubt. And because they're unhappy, they can't help but make everyone around them feel the same way. It's a problem as old as the first sibling rivalry in history, Cain and Abel.

What is the cure? Scripture promises that we have a God who heals the brokenhearted and binds up their wounded hearts. And how does He go about that? He often uses other wounded human beings to convey His love and compassion. Instead of writing people off as lost causes, we need to pray that God will miraculously change them. And we can do something even better. We can pray that God uses us to *become* the miracle for someone else.

Prayer from the Heart

Lord, you tell us to love others. I'll be honest—there are some people that just aren't nice. I don't even like them, and I sure don't want to love them. But I want to please you, so show me how to love the unlovely. Remind me that there are reasons why they act the way they do. Help me to see their hearts—the pain, the hurt, and loneliness that they sometimes use as reasons for their bitterness and hostility. Help me to disarm them with care, love, and patience. Remind me that you loved me with all my flaws and failures. Help me to pass along that love so they'll have the hope that you've so graciously given to me.

∽◌∾

What's on Your Heart Today?

· Why do people sometimes act the way they do?

· How does God heal broken hearts?

· How can you become the person who will love others even when they seem unlovable?

38

SORRY IS THE HARDEST WORD

If it is possible, as much as depends on you,
live peaceably with all men.

ROMANS 12:18 NKJV

"Actually, I've come to apologize.
It's never been easy for me to admit that I'm wrong.
A little bird helped me realize that I have been
insensitive … and selfish … and a whole lot of other
things we don't really need to go into right now."

—*Rosemary Coulter*

*M*inutes after he drove into town, everyone in Hope Valley gathered to admire Lee Coulter's gleaming new Ford. Nobody was more excited than his wife, Rosemary. She told Lee that Dottie Ramsey had hired her at the dress shop and she wanted to make a great impression, so she needed him to drive her to Buxton to buy some taffeta. Lee apologized. He wouldn't be able to do that because he was too busy with work. And then in true Rosemary fashion, she said that wasn't a problem—he could just teach *her* to drive … starting on his lunch break.

Lee tried to teach her the basics, but the first lesson went poorly for Rosemary. Abigail Stanton and Elizabeth Thatcher were visiting at the café when a visibly upset Rosemary staggered in. She admitted that she'd become impatient and decided to drive Lee's car by herself. She'd almost hit Yost's Mercantile … and a wagon … and Katie Brayman's chickens. Lee walked in and confronted her. Things quickly got heated, and to Elizabeth's dismay, Rosemary decided she would be bunking with Elizabeth until stubborn Lee came to his senses.

That night, Elizabeth fought off a headache as Rosemary gabbed nonstop about how unreasonable Lee was being. But then she decided to give Rosemary a dose of hard truth: spouses need to talk through their conflicts and not dig in their heels … or sleep elsewhere. Elizabeth reminded her how blessed she was to have a man like Lee.

For once in her Hope Valley life, Rosemary listened and heeded Elizabeth's advice. She went home and told Lee that she'd been selfish. And wrong. And insensitive. And a whole lot of other things. And then she apologized.

Why is it that admitting we're wrong is so difficult? Why is it so hard to say the words "I'm sorry" to others? How does that go for you? Does your pride make you choke on those words? Maybe it's that we think we're too good to apologize. Or maybe it's because we are insecure, or that we think people will make fun of us. Or perhaps it's because we're afraid they'll reject our apology … or worse … reject us.

But here's the thing, knowing we've hurt someone and that we haven't made it right is a heavy load to handle. But it's an even heavier burden to know we've grieved the heart of God by refusing to forgive someone else. Whether we owe somebody an apology, or they have apologized to us and we've failed to offer them pardon—they're two sides of the same bitter coin. That coin will weigh heavy in our pocket until we dig it out and spend it.

Prayer from the Heart

Lord, you made me, so I know it will come as no surprise to you that I'm as stubborn as a Hope Valley mule sometimes. I don't know why it's so hard for me to admit when I've made a mistake, or why I have such a difficult time saying "I'm sorry" when I have wronged somebody. Please make my heart tender. Dog my conscience until I've righted the situation. Help me to pay attention when you give me those nudges that I need to make amends to someone, and help me to be sincere in my apologies. And when I'm the one who needs to grant forgiveness, remind me of how often you've forgiven me.

⚬⚬⚬

What's on Your Heart Today?

· How can it harm you when you've wronged someone and you won't apologize?

· How does it make you feel after you've done the right thing and made amends to someone?

· Why is forgiveness such a powerful gift?

～ *39* ～

LESS STRESSED, MORE BLESSED

When I am afraid,
I will put my trust in You.
PSALM 56:3 NASB

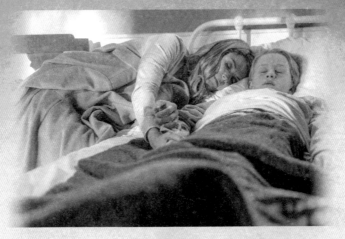

"Miss Thatcher? Brownie wants to stay with you.
He thinks you're sad because of Mountie Jack.
He doesn't want you to worry so much.
Miss Thatcher? Is it true God's watching
over my grandma? Then you don't have to worry.
He's watching over Mountie Jack, too."

—*Opal Weise*

*T*here was a heap of worry going on in Hope Valley. Shane Cantrell stressed about asking Nurse Faith on a date. She worried that his son, Phillip, wouldn't like her. And Phillip fretted he'd be ignored if they became a couple. Kind of a tortured love triangle.

Becky Hastings stressed about her college studies, and was so busy that her brother, Cody, feared she didn't love him anymore. Abigail Stanton worried about Cody. His appetite had been off and he'd seemed tired lately. She panicked later when he came downstairs clutching his abdomen, right before passing out. Then her anxiety skyrocketed—because there was no doctor in town.

Rosemary Coulter stressed because sales weren't exactly booming at Dottie Ramsey's dress shop. And Elizabeth Thatcher fretted about Jack Thornton off in the Northwest Territory fighting the good fight. With every beat of her heart she worried.

Even little Opal Weise was upset. She told Elizabeth her grandmother was ill in Cape Fullerton and her mother was pulling her out of school because they needed to go help her. Elizabeth told Mrs. Weise that Opal could stay with her. Opal was thrilled, but when she couldn't sleep that night, Elizabeth realized she was worried about her sick grandma.

Opal was also worried for Miss Thatcher. She knew she was sad about Mountie Jack being gone to the war. Opal comforted Elizabeth with the truth: just as God was watching over her grandma, she was sure that He was watching over Mountie Jack as well. Wise words from a sweet little girl.

Why are we such good worriers? We fret about what's going to happen or how we're going to make ends meet. We worry about our health, loved ones, and our jobs. But worry doesn't accomplish anything—except to make us feel worse. No amount of regretting can change the past, and no amount of worrying can change the future. As Elizabeth said, "Worrying all the time can drive a person crazy." We make a big mistake when we obsess about our problems instead of fixing our eyes on our problem-solver.

God tells us to bring our burdens to Him, but it's apparent most of us are slow learners in that department. Why does turning our problems over to Him always seem to be a last resort instead of our first response? We worry about the mortgage payment, a broken water heater, or a wayward child, yet our God parted the Red Sea, healed the sick, multiplied five loaves of bread and two fishes into a feast for thousands, and raised the dead. We can trust Him with every detail of our lives, and know that He will always be on time—even when it's not on our timetable.

Prayer from the Heart

Father, I know I shouldn't worry, but I do it every day. I'm tired of carrying these heavy burdens by myself. Remind me that sometimes the answer to my problem hasn't arrived because I haven't taken time to put my needs in your hands. I'm grateful that I can cast all my cares on you. The next time I'm afraid, help me to trust you with whatever I'm facing. Help me to place my worries in your capable hands, to leave them there, and to never try to grab them back. Thank you for being bigger than my circumstances, for being "enough" for whatever I need. Just knowing that you're in charge provides such a sweet, unexplainable peace.

What's on Your Heart Today?

- Why do you worry instead of trusting God?

- How does it affect you when you worry? How does it affect you when you trust God?

- Why should you trust God with your worries?

ᏽ 40 ᏽ

THE TWO GREATEST VIRTUES

So teach us to number our days,
that we may gain a heart of wisdom.

PSALM 90:12 NKJV

"Hope Valley is a place where miracles happen,
where help comes when it's least expected ...
but sometimes, it takes the threat of losing someone
we love to realize how important it is to make
the most of the time we have together."

—*Elizabeth Thatcher*

Cody Hasting's sudden illness affected Hope Valley in multiple ways. It was a wake-up call for his sister, Becky, as his life hung in the balance. She loved her brother, but she'd been so busy with her studies that she'd ignored him.

For Abigail Stanton, those long hours of waiting to see if Cody would survive brought back the memories of the precious moments she had with her late husband, Noah, and son, Peter. Moments that went by way too fast. She begged Cody not to give up, and prayed for God to guide the newly revealed doctor in town, Carson Shepherd, as he performed emergency surgery.

Rosemary Coulter knew that her husband cared about the boy, but Lee just wasn't acting right. It wasn't like him to be ill-natured, distant, or upset with her. When she finally pushed him to be honest with her, he admitted that Cody's illness reminded him of the night his younger brother, Patrick, had died. The boy had asked Lee to read to him from *Tom Sawyer,* but Lee told him he would read to him later. Patrick had slipped away before Lee ever had the chance.

Everyone in town was afraid for Cody. Even the curmudgeonly Henry Gowen, who was spending his days in jail awaiting transfer for his impending trial. He asked interim sheriff, Bill Avery, for a favor. Could he stay in Hope Valley long enough to see the outcome of Cody's surgery? Even Gowen bowed his head in prayer for the boy.

The whole town breathed a collective sigh of relief when Cody woke up from his surgery. His friends sent cards, and he received some special gifts: a baseball bat from his surgeon,

Carson, and from Lee, a treasured copy of *The Adventures of Tom Sawyer* that had once belonged to Patrick. And perhaps the most special gift of all—the official adoption decree from Abigail—now legally his mother.

Elizabeth Thatcher's longing to be reunited with her fiancé, Jack Thornton, and the threat of losing Cody provided valuable lessons to not just Elizabeth and Jack, but for all of the townsfolk—a reminder to trust in God, and to make every moment we have with family and friends the most important priorities in our lives.

In other words, those are the two great virtues of life in Hope Valley. And those same two virtues are what the Bible calls the greatest commandments of life on this little blue ball floating in the cosmos: love God and love others.

You have the power to choose how you live every day of your life. So choose to touch the lives of everyone you meet—for good and for God. Make each day count—on Earth and for all eternity.

Prayer from the Heart

Lord, someday when I'm old, I don't want to look back at my life and see that I've left anything undone. Teach me to live each day as if it might be my last. Open my eyes so that I'll see when my attitude gets off-kilter, or when I've placed things that don't matter in front of the things that are important. I'm thankful that all my days and the measure of my life are in your hands. Remind me that my life is like a vapor that's here for just a moment, and then it fades. Help me to make every day count so that I'll fulfill the purpose and plan that you have for me.

What's on Your Heart Today?

- Why does it often take something like a serious illness to make you truly see things?

- What things really matter in your life?

- How can you gain wisdom when it comes to how you spend your time?

PARTING WORDS

"*H*ope Valley" is as much an idea as it is a place in the world of *When Calls the Heart*. Life brings each of us valleys. But it also brings us an opportunity to turn our heads upward from our valley experiences and look to a God who loves us and who knows His plans for us—plans to prosper us and to give us a *hope* and future.

As we worked on this book, we loved how the God-moments were so evident in every storyline—and if we'll just look for them, we can discover how those moments resonate in our own hearts. The One who wrote the symphonies of our lives has wired all of us with violin strings in our souls—strings tuned to the great themes of sacrifice, courage, nobility, redemption, forgiveness, and resurrection. When stories and ideas and plots pluck those strings, they reverberate with those themes in the very core of our being.

We hope you'll leave the pages of *When God Calls the Heart* with your heart touched in a powerful way, with a new strength to face the circumstances of your life with courage and certainty, and with a deeper appreciation for how God is woven into each day and each moment of your life.

Thank you for traveling on this inspirational journey through four years of life in Hope Valley with us, for catching a glimpse of God in the amazing stories and characters we all love who live there. Through their heartache and despair, through their joys, sorrows, and unexpected situations—and despite their flaws and imperfections—they remained faithful to each other and to God ... and we should do the same.

So hitch up your saddle and get ready for the journey God has for you, because as Elizabeth Thatcher learned when she stepped out in faith to chase her big dreams ... when God calls the heart, you can expect an adventure.

Acknowledgments

M any people are involved in making a book become a reality, and we'd like to express our gratitude to them. Thank you to our publisher, Carlton Garborg, for catching the vision with us. We're grateful to Carol Hatcher for all her help, and to the awesome editing and promotion teams at BroadStreet Publishing.

And to all the people at Motion Picture Corporation of America and Believe Pictures, the production companies behind *When Calls the Heart*, thank you for your generous use of images and storylines. Specifically, Executive Producers Brad Krevoy, Eric Jarboe, and Michael Landon Jr., and Producers Vicki Sotheran and Greg Malcolm, along with four seasons of television's best writers.

Thanks also to the Hallmark Channel, specifically Chief Executive Officer Bill Abbott and Executive Vice President Michelle Vicary, for having the courage to make a family-and-faith series at a time when no other TV network is paying attention to a vastly underserved audience.

And finally, to the creative spirit behind the world of *When Calls the Heart*—Janette Oke. You are the pioneer in faith-based fiction publishing who gave birth to a whole new genre.

Thank you to our prayer team. You're the strength behind all that we do. And to our agent, Tamela Hancock Murray, for all her wise counsel.

We appreciate Jordan Blackstone for granting permission to use four of her Hope Valley paintings in *When God Calls the Heart*. One of them was the basis for the cover. Visit Jordan's website at imaginethatjbphotography.com for more Hope Valley scenes.

As for me (Brian), I want to give loud kudos to my coauthor, Michelle Cox. It was her vision and heavy lifting that even made this book possible, especially on a very rushed schedule. She truly is a very gifted writer and an incredible word-traffic controller!

I also want to thank my beautiful wife of thirty-seven years, Patty, and our five kids for being the glue that holds my life together and empowers me to tell stories and echo eternity in my work. I love you.

I (Michelle) would like to thank my coauthor, Brian Bird, for being such an awesome writing partner. Brian, you made it a joy from start to finish. As a Heartie, I deeply appreciate your commitment to bringing family-friendly entertainment into our homes.

I'd also like to thank my husband, Paul, for praying for me and being so supportive. I love you, and I couldn't do this without you.

Most of all, we want to thank our awesome God who can take a simple conversation at a writers' conference faculty pizza night and turn it into a devotional book and journal.

Finally, thank you to the Hearties—the best fan community for a TV series in all the world. We appreciate you being such loyal supporters of not only *When Calls the Heart* but the values it stands for. We love you!

We appreciate you coming along with us for this project. We've prayed for you, and we hope this book will be a blessing as you discover the God-moments found in Hope Valley ... and in your life.

ABOUT THE AUTHORS

Brian Bird is Executive Producer and Co-Creator of the Hallmark Channel original series *When Calls the Heart*. In his three decades in Hollywood, he has written or produced two dozen films, including most recently, *The Case for Christ*, *Captive*, *Not Easily Broken,* and more than 250 episodes of such shows as *Touched by An Angel*, *Step by Step*, and *Evening Shade*.

His films have garnered awards from the New York Independent Film Festival, New York Festivals, Heartland Film Festival, the Movie Guide Awards, the Telly Awards, and the Christopher Awards.

He has spoken widely on the intersection of the arts and the church, and his professional blog, BrianBird.net, serves as a lively exchange in the best practices of storytelling. Beyond Brian's professional achievements, he considers his top productions to date his thirty-seven-year marriage to wife, Patty, and their five children.

❧❦❧❦

Known for her "encouragement with a Southern drawl," **Michelle Cox** is a speaker and an award-winning, best-selling author. She is a member of the blog team for *Guideposts*, and her "Life with a Southern Grandmother" column runs twice each week at www.Guideposts.org.

She has written for *Focus on the Family*, *FoxNews.com*, *Christian Cinema*, *WHOA Magazine for Women*, *Leading Hearts Magazine,* and the website of Fox News radio host Todd Starnes. Michelle is the creator of the Just 18 Summers® brand of parenting products and resources, and has been a guest on numerous television and radio programs, including *Hannity* and *Focus on the Family*. She and her husband, Paul, have been married for forty-three years, and have three sons, three lovely daughters-in-law, and six perfect grandchildren.

Connect with Michelle at www.just18summers.com, on Twitter @MichelleInspire, and on Facebook at www.Facebook.com/MichelleCoxInspirations.

Look for other *When Calls the Heart*
P R O D U C T S

WHEN CALLS *the* HEART
COOKBOOK

WHEN CALLS *the* HEART
COLORING BOOK

WHEN CALLS *the* HEART
CALENDARS

WHEN CALLS *the* HEART
DVDS

WHEN GOD CALLS
the HEART

When Elizabeth Thatcher followed her dream, hopped on a stage coach, and headed West to become a teacher, one of the things she took with her was her beloved journal. That journal became a treasure, for her, her loved ones, and for future generations who could get to know her, her life lessons, and accumulated wisdom through the words on those pages.

The same is true for us. There's something deeply meaningful about writing down our stories, the moments of our lives, our prayer needs, and chronicling our time spent in study and reflection with God.

Wrapped in exquisite faux leather, this elegant journal features high-quality paper with encouraging quotes. Reflect on the beauty of God, delight in the knowledge of his love for you, and express your thoughts in the space provided.

We're confident that by the time you fill in the last beautiful page, you'll have learned what Elizabeth Thatcher did during her years in Hope Valley. Because when God calls your heart, you can expect an adventure.

Happy writing!

Release Date: February 2018
ISBN: 9781424556182
Faux, 5x8, 160 pages, $16.99